Please return on or before the latest date above.
You can renew online at *www.kent.gov.uk/libs*
or by telephone 08458 247 200

LP
07608   JAMES, E.
                         Max Grant's War

                         MB.

CUSTOMER SERVICE EXCELLENCE

Libraries & Archives

00884\DTP\RN\07.07   LIB 7

HAL GRANT'S WAR

When Hal Grant's father was bushwhacked in the street, it was the opening shot of a range war. Wealthy ranchers were determined to rid Lundon County of its sharecroppers and sodbusters eking out an existence in the marginal lands. Hal should have sided with his fellow ranchers, but he did not believe in mob law. He was caught in the middle — and no one was allowed to sit on the fence in a conflagration that was consuming a county . . .

ELLIOT JAMES

HAL GRANT'S WAR

Complete and Unabridged

LINFORD
Leicester

First published in Great Britain in 2006 by
Robert Hale Limited
London

First Linford Edition
published 2008
by arrangement with
Robert Hale Limited
London

British Library CIP Data

James, Elliot
  Hal Grant's war.—
  Large print ed.—
  Linford western library
  1. Western stories
  2. Large type books
  I. Title
  823.9′2 [F]

  ISBN 978–1–84782–091–4

Published by
F. A. Thorpe (Publishing)
Anstey, Leicestershire

Set by Words & Graphics Ltd.
Anstey, Leicestershire
Printed and bound in Great Britain by
T. J. International Ltd., Padstow, Cornwall

This book is printed on acid-free paper

1

It was about midday and intolerably hot when Hal Grant pulled up his pony and, removing his hat, wiped a shirt-sleeve across his sweating forehead. Narrowing his eyes against the glare of the sun he stared across the relentless flatness of the grasslands.

He was searching the horizon for movement that might indicate the presence of the strays he and four other cowhands were seeking. Seeing nothing that grabbed his immediate attention he uncorked his canteen and took a swig of lukewarm water. Then he slung the canteen and nudged the pony into motion again.

Hal Grant, barely turned twenty, was a tall, broad-shouldered young man with lean waist and hips. He had a square, blunt face that wore a habitual pensive look as if preoccupied with deep thoughts. He had agreed to meet up with the cowhands at a patch of cottonwoods near the beginnings of a group of foothills at the extremity of the Big G range.

'Noon or soon afterwards,' Hal told the little working party. 'We should have come across the steers by then.'

They had set out that morning with high hopes of rounding up the strays and driving the missing stock back to the main range. Now, with the morning gone, Hal Grant had nothing to show for all his riding and vigilance. With a sigh he set his pony on a course that would take him towards the rendez-vous. He hoped the other cowhands had better luck.

After an hour's steady riding he could see the dark smudge on the horizon indicating the clump of cotton-woods that was his rendezvous. Hal yawned prodigiously. It had been a long and tiring morning, made more so by the lack of success in locating the missing stock. He noted a dust trail

2

parallel to his own and reckoned his hands were gathering at the meeting-place.

The cowboys were waiting for him as arranged. They had been squatting in a little group engaged in conversation when he rode up.

'Howdy, Hal.'

Hal nodded a greeting and swung down, glad for the opportunity to stretch his legs. Even though he was the boss's son and would eventually take over the Big G ranch from his father, Harry Grant, the cowboys in his father's pay treated Hal as an equal. He was ever one of them, ready for a game of cards, a drink and joke and a yarn by the camp-fire.

'Any sign?' he asked.

No one answered and Hal looked sharply at the men. There was something in their expressions that warned him — a hint of news he was not going to like.

'Come on, spit it out, what is it?'

'Charlie here, found sign, tracks

leadin' towards Peterstown.'

Hal stared bleakly at the men. Peterstown was a mish-mash of land-claims that had been granted by government to settlers wanting to establish farms and smallholdings.

Hal had only heard rumours of the hardships endured by the settlers. The land was too dry for crops and they had not sufficient acreage to establish animal husbandry in enough numbers to make the venture viable. Most of the settlers existed on the meagre veg-etables and corn they grew near their hovels. Some would have a dairy-cow or a few goats to add milk to their diet. For most it was a miserable hand-to-mouth existence.

'When you say tracks, what you talkin' about?'

'It's a sizeable herd, Hal. I would say eighty to a hundred head.'

Hal swore long and profanely. He knew the odd steer was culled from his herds by desperate and starving home-steaders and accepted that. To try and apprehend the culprits of such petty thieving would be a waste of time and resources. Rustling on this scale was a more serious matter.

'You think this is the first time?'

Hal Grant looked at John Ollinger for an answer. Ollinger, a grizzled old-timer, had been with the Big G for many years. The man was an experienced cowhand and Hal Grant valued his advice. Ollinger shifted the habitual wad of tobacco in his mouth and spat a thin, brown stream. Hal waited patiently. The old-timer never spoke without weighing his words first.

'My guess it's been goin' on for some time. That's why this area is so darn thin on cattle.'

'When do you reckon this lot was lifted?'

'Charlie here reckons last night sometime. It was him as found the sign.'

The men waited patiently while Hal mulled this over.

'You men go on back to the Big G

and tell Pa about this. Charlie, you point me at that trail and then you can go hightail it back to join them.'

Hal gathered up his reins and waited for the cowhands to obey his instructions. No one moved. They stood by their mounts, staring up at the young straw-boss of the biggest ranch in the area.

'You heard me. What's holdin' you fellas?'

'What you aimin' to do, Hal?' Ollinger countered.

Hal regarded the old-timer, knowing this was a man who was loyal to the Big G and hard-working to boot.

'I aim to follow that herd an' catch up with them there rustlers, that's what.'

'You thinkin' of goin' alone?'

'Sure, I can handle me a few rustlers.'

'No siree, you ain't goin' on your own.' Ollinger swung on to his pony. 'I guess I'd better ride along with you, case you get lost.'

'John, there's likely to be trouble.'

'Trouble . . . mmnn . . . that's even more reason for me to tail along.'

By now everyone was mounted and waiting expectantly.

'There may be shootin', boys,' Ollinger was addressing the remaining three cowhands. 'You fellas want a cut of the action?'

There was a chorus of accord.

'Will you fellas just do for once what I tell you to do?'

'You hear that, boys? Young Hal here wants us to ride along with him,' Ollinger said, his back to Hal. 'Ready when you are, boss.'

Hal Grant sighed, knowing it was useless to argue with his crew in this mood. Whatever he said they would agree with and then do the opposite. 'All right, then have it your way. Check your weapons.'

Hal pulled his own six-shooter and examined the rounds in the cylinder. The weapon had been a birthday present from his father on his eighteenth birthday. Charlie Morton, a youngish cowhand with a freckled face, who had spotted the tracks of the stolen cattle, carried a Winchester as well as his sidearm. Francisco Gonzales, a young Mexican cowhand, also had a carbine. Harvey Baker, a surly middle-aged man, was the fifth member of the little band.

Five armed cowboys should be able to handle a few rustlers, Harry surmised.

'OK, boys,' Harry said. 'Let's go and get those beeves back.'

2

Judging by the trail left by the rustled herd Hal guessed the cowboy's estimate of the steers driven off had been correct. In fact he thought there were maybe upwards of a hundred or more cattle stolen.

'Looks like they're drivin' them into the Dunlop Hills,' Ollinger commented, indicating the range of low hills that loomed in the distance.

Hal nodded. 'They'll think to hole up somewheres an' alter the Big G brand before sellin' them on. All right, boys, some of you drop back an' follow behind. I want twenty or thirty yards between each rider. No point in bunchin' up an' givin' them an easy target just in case they see us before we spot them.'

The trail was an easy one to follow. A bunch of a hundred or so steers churned up enough dust and earth for even the most inexperienced rider to follow. Hal was riding in the lead with his riders strung out behind him. The shot when it came took them all by surprise. Hal kicked his spurs and headed for a bunch of cottonwood trees.

He did not look behind to see what his cowhands were doing but he assumed the men would be going to ground. A few more shots were sent out and Hal, even as he was urging his mount forward, was searching the terrain ahead in an effort to spot the shooter.

Hal reached the cover of the trees and dropped from his mount. With a swift flick he twisted the reins over a branch and then scrambled through the trees to scan the area he estimated the shots were coming from.

The ambusher had chosen his location well. Hal had been crossing flats towards a break in the hills. He had been keeping an eye on the trail and scanning ahead from time to time for any sign of their quarry. Now he and his men were stopped dead in their tracks. Hal fumed at the delay. He turned and searched for any sign of his cowhands. Like him they had gone to ground.

'Where the hell's Charlie with that Winchester,' he muttered. At this distance only another rifle could answer the one holed up in the rocks ahead.

Now that the gunman had no target to aim at the shots had ceased. Suddenly there was a flurry of rifle shots from behind Hal as Charlie opened up from cover. At the same time a horse raced forward. With some surprise, Hal saw it was John Ollinger urging his mount towards the rocks ahead.

The marksman began firing at the rider. Hal immediately spotted the position of the rifleman and so did Charlie. He began peppering the area with rifle fire. Hal raced for his mount. He could not let his cowboys take all the risks.

He burst from the cover of the trees and directed his pony towards the gunman's estimated position. Zigzagging his agile cowpony to make a more difficult target, he had his pistol in hand but did not fire. He needed to conserve his firepower till he was close enough for a better shot at the ambusher.

With two targets to work on and another marksman making him keep his head down, the man in the rocks was having a difficult time deciding what was the greatest threat. After only a few shots fired off wildly the man must have realized the riders would soon be upon him. As Hal drew near the gunman's position he saw a figure rise up and fire off a couple of hurried shots, then run back to where he had his mount tethered.

Hal snapped off a few shots at the man. He knew there was little chance of a hit. He fired only to hurry the ambusher on his way. Further to the right of him Ollinger also opened up. Horse and rider suddenly appeared, riding hard. Hal emptied his revolver towards the tempting target. To his surprise the running horse stumbled and went down, throwing the rider. Behind him Ollinger whooped and spurred past Hal. Shaking his head at the keen courage of the old-timer Hal followed closely behind.

The ambusher's horse was on its feet but seemed to be favouring one of its hindlegs. The man who had shot at them was sitting on the ground nursing a busted shoulder along with a bruised and bleeding face.

'Keep him covered.' Hal called an unnecessary warning to Ollinger, who was sitting his horse with his pistol aimed at the injured man. 'OK, mister, on your feet, you ain't that bad injured.'

The man stayed where he was, glaring up at his captors. Hal figured he was in his early twenties — a chubby-faced young man with thin lips and mean, pinched eyes. There was the clatter of hoofs as the remainder of Hal's party caught up with them.

'Get his weapons,' Hal called.

Francisco recovered a Colt .45 and a Remington rifle along with a wicked-looking Bowie before hauling the man to his feet.

'OK, fella, what's the idea shootin' at us?'

'I thought you were aimin' to bush-whack me. I weren't takin' any chances.'

'You one of the gang as took a herd of beeves off our range?'

'Beeves! I ain't seen no beeves. What beeves you on about?'

'Don't know why you bother questio-nin' this lyin' gopher, might as well string him up now,' said Harvey Baker. 'He was left to cover the back trail while his pals made off with our cattle.'

'Damn good idea,' agreed Ollinger. 'One thing I hate is a no-account, murderin' rustler.'

'You can't hang me! I was just ridin' home mindin' my own business when you fellas suddenly come on my back trail. How do I know you ain't rustlers yourselves?'

'What's your moniker, fella?' Hal asked. 'We need a name to put on your grave marker.'

The man looked scared for the first time. 'Name's Craig Huston, I come from a respectable family. You'll be hangin' an innocent man.'

'Rope him to his horse,' Hal instructed. 'We'll take him with us.'

'That horse is in a bad way, Hal. Looks like it took a bullet in its hind leg. That's why it went down.'

Hal saw the blood running down the animal's leg.

'Guess we'll have to leave him here for now. Collect him on the way back. He ain't goin' nowhere with a lamed horse. What's the wound like, John?'

'Looks like he busted his shoulder.'

'Not the man, damnit, I mean the horse!'

'Oh, sorry, boss, doesn't look too bad. If we get the bullet out and he's rested up a mite he should heal up good.'

'Well, we'll take care of it on the way

back. Let's press on and catch up with the rest of the rustlers. Can't be that far ahead now.'

'I say string him up now,' muttered Baker.

Hal ignored the mean-tempered Baker and headed his mount into the hills.

3

It was dusk before they sighted the herd. By then they were aware that they would be sleeping under the stars that night. They were too far from the home range to expect to return before nightfall. Hal called his riders together for a conference.

'Ollinger, I want no more of that reckless behaviour. You could have got yourself shot rushin' that rifleman,' he admonished the old-timer.

'Hell, young Hal.' Ollinger had crooked his leg over his pommel and busied himself cutting a fresh plug of tobacco. 'I had no intention of riskin' my life like you just said I did. This old nag of mine she took fright at all that shootin' an' just took off. I couldn't hold her back. Sure scared the shit outta me, her runnin' like that.' He shook his head in mock despair. 'Man

17

my age ought to be takin' it easy, not takin' risks to life and limb.'

Hal looked sceptically at the man, not believing him for a minute. It was most unlikely an experienced hand like Ollinger would allow his horse to bolt. 'Well, just bear in mind there are four of us to spare them there old limbs of yours.' He cast an eye around at his grinning riders. 'That goes for you lot as well. Right, this is the plan. We follow the herd till they bed down for the night. I reckon they have come so far as to believe they are safe for now. When it's dark enough we drift on up to the herd. Once we've spotted the night-guard one of us will mosey on in. If challenged we call out Craig Huston's name. That should throw them off guard and then we shouldn't have too much trouble takin' them down. Between us we should manage. Every-one clear what to do?'

'Sure, boss, should be as easy as ropin' dogies.'

'I hope,' said Hal fervently. 'No

shootin'. Once we have the drop on them they should be easy prey.'

There were no more stops and no one seemed inclined to talk as they followed the herd at a respectable distance. The men were weary from being on the go from early sunup with no meal-breaks. The dusk was dropping steadily, as were their eyelids. Sleeping in the saddle was not unusual for cowboys on long watches.

After what seemed interminable hours following in the wake of the herd a change in the movements ahead was sensed. The little party of horsemen drew rein and sat their horses, eyes straining into the distance.

'Looks like they're beddin' down for the night,' Hal at last ventured. 'Let's give them an hour or so to allay suspicion an' then we'll move in. Get some rest. I'll keep watch while you get your heads down.'

They loosened girths and ground-tethered the mounts. Up ahead the dark mass they had been following remained in place. There was not a breath of wind. The moon was sailing high, bathing the terrain in a soft, silver radiance. Shadows were etched stark and sharp on the dark earth. Silence pressed down like an enveloping sheet, masking sounds from far off. The stars were bright pinpricks in the taut canvas of the sky. It was a night of peace and tranquillity. Used to sleeping under the stars, the men stretched out on the earth and slept.

★　★　★

Cautiously they moved forward. Hal was tense as he tried to see ahead. He was worried in case the rustlers had placed a guard on the back trail. Then he saw the flickering light from the fire. He pointed ahead.

'One of you mosey on round the herd and find out if they've posted a night-herder. Remember, you're Craig Huston.' He had a sudden thought and revised his instructions. 'No, forget that. Call out that Craig hasn't returned and someone has to go look for him. That should get you in close enough to him without rousing his suspicions. An' remember, no shootin'. The quieter we operate the safer it'll be for all of us.'

Harvey Baker edged his mount forward.

'I'll take the night-guard,' he volunteered.

'Give us time to get to the camp,' Hal instructed. 'And remember Harvey, no shootin'.'

He watched the man and horse fade into the night and wondered whether he was wise in letting the mean-tempered Baker take the most delicate part of the operation. By then it was too late to change his mind.

'Let's go.'

They moved forward steadily, angling towards the firelight.

'We'll walk the last piece,' Hal muttered.

Holding reins in one hand and with weapons out the little band of cowboys moved in on the rustler camp. About fifty yards out they had still not been detected.

'Spread out,' Hal whispered. So far so good, he thought.

They could see the shapes of two men stretched out on the ground wrapped in their blankets. Two more were sitting cross-legged facing each other. They seemed engrossed in a game of cards. Hal let go the reins of his horse. They would soon be close enough to call on the men to surrender.

The shots when they came were loud and violent in the stillness of the night. The men in the camp reacted immediately. They were on their feet and Hal groaned as he realized all hope of surprise had vanished with those shots. His premonitions about Harvey Baker had been correct. Then more shots rang out. Throwing caution to the wind Hal ran forward.

'Throw down your guns, you men. We have you surrounded.'

He flung himself to the earth as he

saw the gun flashes from the camp.

'Goddamn that Harvey!' Hal moaned to no one in particular. He fired over the heads of the silhouettes in the camp. Around him his own men opened up. Hal saw one of the rustlers spin round and fall.

'Goddamn it, aim over their heads,' he yelled. He was not sure his men would heed him, for a virtual hail of lead was hurling out from the rustlers' camp. Someone kicked the fire apart and the flames died to a low flickering. Hornets of lead spun past his head and out into the night.

'Hell an' damn it,' Hal swore. What should have been a straightforward confrontation had developed into a firefight.

The shooting rendered the night into a hellish mixture of noise and gunflashes. Not knowing what else to do, Hal stayed where he was and made his own contribution to the noise and confusion. He was firing wide, hoping the men defending the camp might still surrender.

Right now there was no let-up in their firepower. Bullets continued to pour from the camp. Around him Hal could see his own hands returning the fire. Just when Hal thought things could not get any worse the cattle decided to add their own brand of havoc to the night. Terrified by the barrage of shots, with a great bellowing and roaring the herd swung into motion. Instinctively they turned in the direction of the home range.

Hal heard the bawling and then the earth began to vibrate beneath him. In spite of the bullets whistling past him he leap to his feet and looked round for his mount. It was nowhere to be seen. His horse, usually so well behaved and trained to wait for its master, had taken off into the night. Hal looked round frantically. The dark tide of bellowing steers was sweeping out of the night towards him and he was afoot.

4

Murphy's Emporium was a hotel, general stores, undertakers and dance-hall. On the walls of the building all these services were advertised in foot-high lettering: EAT — DRINK — SLEEP — DANCE — BUY A SHOVEL AND BE BURIED BY MURPHY. As the visitors entered the hotel foyer, painted arrows directed the prospective customer towards the service he was most in need of.

On the night that Hal Grant and his cowpokes were having bother with rustlers a meeting was being assembled to discuss those very difficulties.

Murphy's dance-hall was the place where the Wyoming Ranchers' Institute held their monthly meetings. The dance-hall was big enough to hold the forty or so members who were expected to attend. The ranch bosses would often bring along their top hands and foremen to sit in on the important meetings and these could swell the numbers to sixty or more. These hired men were very often a repository of local lore and frequently knew more about what went on in the area than did the ranch owners themselves.

Another advantage of the dance-hall was the services the big Irishman provided. He laid on waiters to attend on the tables set out for the large crowd of hard-drinking men who attended the institute's meetings. Food and alcohol could be ordered and delivered direct to the table. And at the end of the night's business, girls could be hired to help the men relax. Often business deals worth thousands were hatched amongst the conviviality of such meetings.

Harry Grant, Hal's father, was a senior member of the institute. He regularly attended the meetings and was well-respected as a voice of good sense and seasoned judgement. The owner of the emporium was an Irishman named Stump Murphy. As well as businesses in town he had his own ranch, the Lazy M that was run for him by a straw boss, Ronald Preston. Preston was a tough, surly individual with a mean disposition. His only saving grace was his undivided loyalty to his boss.

'Order, I call this meeting to order.' Big Joe Truslow tried to call the meeting to order. As chairman, Murphy sat near Truslow, watching the faces of the cowmen, smiling at his friends and letting his glance slide over those he disliked. One man he intensely disliked was Harry Grant.

Some of this dislike came from jealousy. Harry Grant owned the biggest and richest ranch in the territory and Stump Murphy resented the clout Harry wielded amongst the cattlemen. He had further cause for dislike, as Harry was most likely to oppose any scheme involving violence put forward by Murphy. Harry Grant believed in settling disputes peacefully and violence was the court of last resort. Murphy's nature was to lash out at those he considered weaker than himself in order to obtain his ends.

'Order!'

Truslow took out his six-shooter and used it as a gavel. The hubbub of noise subsided. The next period was taken up with the reading of the minutes from the last meeting and general news from around the region. Beef-and feed-prices were discussed briefly, along with their effects on the marketing of cattle. When the regular items were cleared it was the turn of Stump Murphy to rise and address the assembly.

'You know what we have gathered here today to discuss. There is a plague in this county. That plague is rustlin'. All of you have been touched by this plague. There is a steady drain on our herds from the scum who inhabit Peterstown. What we have today in Peterstown is a state of anarchy. We hardworkin' ranchers have built up legitimate businesses. The inhabitants of Peterstown are leeches battenin' on the backside of our society. We catch a rustler and take him in to the county court. What happens?' Murphy banged his fist on the table on front of him. The decanter of water and the glasses jolted and chimed briefly. 'You all know what happens. The rustlers are acquitted. I have lost scores of beeves to those thievin' scumbags. I have resorted to the law for redress. What do I get for my patience and law-abidin' patience? I tell you what I get. I get a rustler set free again. Free to go on rustlin'. They say crime does not pay. I say crime does pay if you are livin' in Lundon County. Well, fellow-ranchers, I for one have had enough.'

Murphy paused to pour himself a drink from the decanter. He drank deeply, all the while trying to assess what effect his words were having on his listeners. He could see men nodding in agreement and some in earnest conversation as they discussed the implications of his speech. Murphy set the glass down and leaned forward with his knuckles on the table. He thrust his neck forward like a bull eyeing up rivals he might have to take on for domination of the herd.

'I for one have had enough of thievin'. I run my ranch as a business. I am not a charity. I say, if a man can't make a go of it in this country with honest toil then he has no place in this country.'

Again the big man paused. The Irishman was a veritable giant. He had massive breadth of shoulders. The broadcloth suits he favoured seemed too small to contain his huge frame. He had a mop of wiry black hair and dark, full eyebrows. The face was full-blown with a blunt, broad nose and wide expressive mouth. His general demeanour was of a big, easy-going man with a ready smile. Hidden beneath the genial *bonhomie* was a streak of brutality.

'Let me tell you a story about the old

country. I was born of good Protestant stock. My family farmed the land an' prospered. Our poorer neighbours were jealous of our success. Instead of workin' hard and makin' their land fertile they took the lazy way out an' stole from their hardworkin' neighbours. The devils picked isolated farms and raided for food, cattle an' sometimes in their foraging they murdered when they were caught in the act. What did the honest people do? I tell you what we did. We took the law into our own hands. We formed together an' called ourselves the Vindicators.' Murphy held up a huge clenched fist, for all the world like a knotted piece of hickory. 'Each of us was armed with an axe. We knew who the thieves were. What did we do with the axes? I tell you what we did. We chopped off the right hand. That's the hand he uses to thieve with. And then we plunged the stump into a pot of boiling pitch. That way he would live on as a witness — a witness that crime did not pay. That's what we did.'

The big man paused again for effect. Suddenly the significance of Stump Murphy's nickname was borne home to the audience and a ripple of laughter ran through the crowd. Suddenly someone started clapping. With a sudden surge of enthusiasm the ranchers rose to their feet clapping wildly. Murphy stood beaming down at the men endorsing him so ardently. He stood proudly, like a king accepting homage from his subjects, allowing the applause to run its course. Eventually the men subsided, talking excitedly. With a theatrical gesture Stump Murphy produced some folded sheets of paper from his inside pocket and waved these in the air.

'Here is a list of names. All the names on this list are known cattle-thieves. Some don't steal directly but maybe buy stolen beeves or take them in lieu of payment for goods or services. There are sixty-six names on this piece of paper.'

The sheets were held up and moved around in an arc so that every man in the room could see the documents.

'I'm not proposin' the axe an' pitch treatment for these men. No, something more permanent is needed. I'm proposin' we hang every name on this list. That's the only way to stamp out rustlin' in Lundon County.'

This time the applause was even more noisy and prolonged.

5

Out of the noise and dust of the rustlers' camp came the horsemen, galloping wildly to escape the stampeding herd. Hal was about to start running even though he knew it was hopeless to try and outrun the charging cattle. Seeing the fleeing rustlers gave him an even better idea, but one that was fraught with as much danger.

The outlaws were approaching rapidly, their horses panicked by the maddening noise of many hoofs behind them. Hal crouched in readiness. He knew there was slim chance that he would succeed in what he was about to attempt. Then the nearest rider was almost on him.

With a sudden wild leap Hal flung himself up and waved his arms about his head while at the same time yelling at the top of his voice. Horse and rider tried to swerve. The rider was almost unseated but held on.

Hal grabbed for a stirrup strap. His arm was almost torn from its socket but he held on and using the momentum of the horse bounced his feet on the earth. By sheer strength he managed to get one leg hooked over the horse. Clinging desperately to the rider's shirt he hauled himself on to the madly plunging horse. The rider was so engaged in trying to control his panic-stricken mount he had no time to fight off the crazy man now clinging to his back. Hal wrapped his arms round the man's waist and clung tight. The horse plunged on with the double load, eager to escape the bellowing nemesis rapidly trying to overtake them.

Clinging tight to his unwilling rescuer Hal risked a glance over his shoulder. The herd was slowly gaining. Hal yelled at the rider to go faster. There was a sudden roar and a flash from under the man's arm and something hot and lethal tore into Hal's side.

The shock and pain was such that he almost lost his precarious hold on the back of the speeding animal. Desperately he clung on, the agony made worse by the violent movement of the mount. The pistol in the man's hand roared again. Luckily for Hal this time the bullet passed harmlessly into the night.

Hal let go his hold on the man's waist and grabbed instead for the hand that was holding the pistol. His fingers encountered the warm metal of the weapon. In an effort to discourage the man from firing again he pushed as hard as he could forwards and inwards. When the gun fired again this time the bullet went somewhere into the groin of the rustler. Hal heard the man scream, and then slump forward. With his side on fire Hal held grimly on as best he could.

The rider lost control of his mount, his body flopping loosely forward. Fortunately the horse raced on in wild panic anxious to keep ahead of the herd thundering in its wake. It was only by a supreme effort of will and sheer strength that Hal kept the injured rider upright. He knew if the man flopped to one side there was every danger they would both be thrown from the racing horse. That was the beginning of a nightmare ride for Hal.

The night was filled with the thunder of the charging herd. His side ached intolerably and his muscles screamed for release from the relentless pressure of keeping himself and the injured rider on top of the madly racing horse. Hal inched his good hand down the body of his partner in this nightmare ride, searching for the reins. He had to keep a grip on the dead weight of the man while at the same time feeling for the reins. At last he encountered the leather bands still clasped in the injured man's hands. He grasped the leathers and began the onerous task of pulling the horse's head to the left.

The horse felt the tugging and began to respond. Slowly, painfully slowly, the pony changed direction so that it was still running ahead but at an angle to the oncoming herd. Hal was hoping to pull far enough to the side to allow the herd to run past.

On they thundered into the night. Hal's body was a numbed vessel of pain and tension. He could do nothing more. He had to hang on and try to keep himself and the injured rustler in the saddle. All the while he was hoping the horse would eventually run wide enough to escape the oncoming hoofs of the maddened cattle.

There was another danger that he did not dare think about, and that was a stumble in the night for his mount. He knew if that happened he would be finished, for he had not the strength to escape once on the ground again. He gritted his teeth against the pain and held on, not knowing if he was supporting a wounded man or if his companion in this crisis was dead.

★　★　★

Harry Grant stepped out into the night air of Lourdes. He was angry. In spite of his pleas to his fellow members of the Wyoming Ranchers' Institute to reject Murphy's murderous plan they were going down that road anyway.

He and Murphy had never seen eye to eye. Harry knew the man was a bully and could not hide the contempt he felt for the big Irishman. In the past they had clashed over policy in the institute meetings. Harry had always won the arguments, for Murphy was never able to face Harry down. Now it looked as if Murphy had carried the weaker sections of the members with him.

Ignoring the malevolent posturing of Murphy, Harry had made his objections loud and clear.

'Murphy tells you we are livin' in anarchy. I tell you this. If we go along with his plan we really will be livin' in anarchy. The law of the gun will prevail. Not one of you will be safe. Not one of you will be immune from the lawlessness of the Colt. Nor indeed if you follow this mad Irishman will your families be safe.

'Believe you me, I have seen that happen right here in Lundon County before it ever reached the status of county. An' who is to tell if the men on this so-called death list are guilty. How do we know that this is not some mad scheme dreamed up by a few men to rid themselves of enemies who have wronged them. I say, go down the path of law. It might take a little longer but it is much safer for the health of this community.'

The vote had been taken and Harry had lost the argument.

Harry's eye had fixed Murphy with an intent look. 'I shall fight you over this, Murphy. If I have to go to the governor I will take it upon myself to inform him of the state of affairs in his territory.'

It was as he stepped from the boardwalk the shots came from each side. One hit him in the side and one hit him in the chest. Harry Grant went down but even as he fell his own Colt was in his hand. With pain-glazed eyes he fired towards the gun-flashes. There was the sound of running feet and the assassins fled leaving Harry Grant bleeding in the street.

6

On the same night that Harry Grant was shot in the streets of Lourdes his son Hal fell from the back of his exhausted mount. The injured rider he had kept in the saddle tumbled to the ground and lay ominously still. Somewhere out to his right the stampeding herd thundered on its way.

For long moments Hal lay where he had landed. He had the presence of mind to keep a tight hold on the reins of the horse. His side was on fire where the bullet from the rustler had penetrated. The muscles of his body were cramping as the pressure of holding his seat on the bolting pony was slowly released.

'Ooh,' he groaned as waves of agony washed over him. 'Maybe it would have been easier to have allowed the steers to trample me.'

Slowly he sat up, favouring his wound. He undid his bandanna and stuffed it inside his shirt to cover the wound and soak up the blood. Only when he had tended to his own needs did he turn his attention to the downed rustler. As he did so the last of the herd thundered past and vanished into the dust-shrouded night.

'At least they're headed back to home range,' Hal informed the unresponsive outlaw.

By the light of a bright moon he examined the man. As he pressed his hands down along the body searching for the wound he found a wet patch starting just above the belt-buckle. He guessed the bullet had gone in sideways and traversed through the man's guts. With such a wound Hal wondered if the man could survive.

Hal looked around him but to all intents and purposes they were alone on this deserted place. Worried the horse might take off he tied the reins to the rustler's boot. There was nothing much he could do for the wounded man. He had no materials to stanch the bleeding. The man had taken off into the night ahead of the herd in too much of a hurry even to strap on his bedroll.

There was a canteen tied on the saddle and Hal helped himself to that. Then he endeavoured to give some to the wounded man. He tried to remember all he knew about stomach wounds. They weren't supposed to take any drinks. He knew also not many survived a gut shot. He felt hopelessly inadequate as he wondered what to do for the best.

'Goddamn it, fella, I sure don't know what to do to help. Why'd you have to take up cattle-rustlin' anyways?'

When the man spoke it startled Hal. 'Maurice . . . is that you?'

'What you say, fella? I ain't Maurice. My name's Hal Grant. I sure am sorry you got shot.'

'Is it bad?' The words were barely audible.

'I don't think so. When my men come

by I'll send for help. We'll get you patched up good as new again.'

There was silence again and Hal was more afraid now the wounded man had spoken to him. For some reason he felt responsible for the man's sorry condition. He was cold and shivering as his own wound nagged him. Suddenly a hand reached out and grabbed Hal with surprising strength.

'You're not Maurice.'

'No fella, I ain't Maurice. Was he one of the fellas as stole those cattle?'

There was another long silence before the man spoke again.

'Will you get word to my family? Tell them what happened. This was my first time rustlin'. Maurice told me it was easy money. I needed the money bad.' The hand that was gripping Hal's arm loosened slightly. 'You will tell my family. Don't tell them how it really was. Say I was set upon and robbed. Will you do that for me, fella?'

'Ain't no use you talkin' like that. You

45

can tell them yourself when we get you home.'

'I ain't goin' home, fella. What you say your name was?'

'Hal. You can call me Hal.'

'Hal . . . I got no feelin' down there. Can't move my legs. An' I'm cold . . . so cold. Hal, would you say a prayer for me? I don't know much prayin' myself. It might help if you said it for me.'

Hal desperately racked his brains for a prayer. His mother sometimes read from the Bible to the family in the evening. 'Hear my prayer, O Lord, and let my cry come unto thee. Hide not your face from me when I am in trouble. Incline thine ear unto me in the night when I call upon you. You are my light and revelation . . . ' Hal faltered to a halt, his memory failing.

'That's good . . . Hal . . . you will tell my ma an' my kid brother?'

'Where you from? I'll get word to them.'

'Missus Josephine Hendron, she lives

on Grand Hill farm. Don't tell her her son James was a rustler . . . promise me . . . '

The hand relaxed its grip on Hal's arm and he heard a long deep sigh from the wounded man. Cautiously he leaned over and placed his ear to the man's chest. Then he sat back and in spite of his own plight he felt immensely sad for the life just over.

'God giveth and God taketh away. Ashes to ashes and dust to dust. May your soul rest in the Lord, James Hendron. I promise I will carry the sad news to your family.'

He fumbled with the reins and released them from the dead man's boot. Wearily he climbed to his feet. With some effort he climbed on to the horse.

He was thankful the animal had calmed down once the terror of the stampeding herd had passed. Hal swayed in the saddle, pain radiating out from his side, threatening to overwhelm him. He felt around the saddle and found the dead rustler's lariat. With this he roped himself in place atop the saddle. With one last look at the lifeless figure stretched out on the ground he set the pony to follow the herd.

7

'Hal, Hal, what the hell's happened to you? Christ, man, you been hurt.'

'Get a blanket on the ground there. Let's have a look at that there wound.'

Hands were lifting him from the saddle.

'What happened, Hal? Can you hear me? Are you hurt bad?'

'There's blood all down his side and on his pants.'

'Looks like he's been shot.'

The voices went on around him. He floated in and out of consciousness.

'Looks like it stopped bleeding. Helluva lot of blood though. Looks like someone roped him on the horse an' sent him on his way.'

'Sure looks in a bad way. We better get him back to the ranch.'

'Tear some strips from that blanket and bind it tight around him. That way it shouldn't start bleedin' again.'

After they had trussed him with the makeshift bandages the pain lessened somewhat.

'Drink . . . ' he croaked, 'water . . . '

'Sure, Hal.'

The canteen was taken from his lips while he was still sucking down the life-giving water.

'Maybe shouldn't drink so much what with being shot an' all.'

He felt himself being lifted back on the horse again and the slow, painful ride to the ranch began.

★   ★   ★

When he came to his mother was by his bedside. She looked pale and tired. Her eyes were swollen and red from weeping. He smiled wanly at her.

'Thought you'd lost me, Ma. Well, I ain't that easy to kill.'

The tears flooded down her cheeks and he thought they were tears of relief at his awakening. He reached out and took her dainty hand in his big work-hardened one. When she spoke her voice was muffled and hesitant, as if she were labouring under a great burden of grief.

'Doc Patterson says you were lucky. The bullet passed through and touched nothing vital. He says you rest easy and the wound will heal clean.'

He smiled reassuringly at her. Her face was puffy from weeping. She was still an attractive woman even though she had streaks of grey hair and crow's feet were spreading out from the corners of her eyes. She looked down at his hand holding hers. Then she raised the hand and, kissing it, held it against her cheek for a moment.

'It's your pa, Hal,' she murmured indistinctly.

He frowned at her. 'Pa, he take it bad then?'

The tears were flowing hard now. 'He's been shot, Hal.' She could speak no more for she broke down then and sobbed. Hal made an effort to sit up.

His wounded side pulled painfully. He winced but ignored the pain as he gathered her to him.

'Oh God, Ma, is it bad?'

He watched her grey head nod emphatically. Her wide tearful eyes stared at him. She could not speak.

He did not question her further. He just held her and let her sob her heart out. The door opened and Hal's younger brother John poked his head in the room. John and Hal stared at each other for long moments before John slid into the room. He came over and rested his hand on his mother's bowed shoulders. She pulled herself upright and mopped at her eyes with a sodden handkerchief.

'Pa's been askin' for Hal. I ain't told him you been hurt.'

Hal felt his world was spinning out of kilter. His mother's outpouring of grief and his brother's face bore an unreal testimony to the seriousness of his father's injuries. Harry Grant was larger than life. Hal could not quite grasp what his family was trying to tell him.

'I'd better go an' see Pa.' He eased himself to the edge of the bed. 'Help me with my trousers, John.'

The short journey down the corridor to his father's bedroom seemed interminably long and painful. Hal was light-headed and full of foreboding. When eventually he did see his father lying in his bed with waxen features he was shocked.

'Remember, Hal, he don't know you been shot,' John whispered. He eased Hal into the chair beside the head of the bed.

'Pa, it's me, Hal. You wanted to see me.'

'Hal.' The eyes opened. 'I been waitin' for you.' The voice was barely above a whisper. 'You find them strays?'

'Sure, Pa. Had a mite of trouble. Rustlers had took them, but we got them back.'

A faint smile appeared on the pale lips. 'That's my boy.' Harry Grant turned his head slightly and looked at his son. 'It's all yours now. You got to take over the runnin' of the Big G.'

'Pa, that's foolish talk. You'll be up an' around in a while.'

'I worried about you, Hal,' Harry Grant went on, ignoring his son's observation. 'You were pretty wild an' got mixed up in some sorry company but I believe you left all that behind.'

Hal nodded, not wanting to think of his wild antics a few years back when he had mixed with an unsavoury crowd at the Mule's Head tavern.

'I was a mite foolish, Pa, but I learned my lesson.'

There was silence for a while between them. Then Hal asked the question that had been burning in him since he learned about his father's injury.

'Who did it, Pa, who shot you?'

'Didn't see, son. Shot out of the dark at me. Have a good guess but only speculation.' There was silence for another moment or two. 'Had a run-in with Stump Murphy at the institute. Wants to set up a vigilante gang. He has a list of people they gonna kill. I said no. I said I would fight them all the way. Things got pretty heated. Coulda been anyone as had a grudge against me, or even mistaken identity. No matter about that. What's done is done. Just you watch your back.' Harry Grant subsided into silence.

Hal sat by the bedside staring at his father's sunken frame. He had believed his father would always be there. He was as solid and permanent as the Big G. His father was silent so long Hal thought he had slipped away.

'Pa.'

Harry Grant's eyes opened. 'All hell's gonna break out, Hal. With me out of the way Murphy will push the institute into doin' what he wants. Stay out of it, Hal. Keep the Big G out of the trouble that's comin'. Them homesteaders won't sit still and allow themselves to be murdered. This will be a war to shake the county. Lot of innocent people will be killed. Your job is to keep the Big G safe.' Harry Grant's hand reached out and searched for Hal's. The hand was cold but there was enough strength to squeeze gently. 'Call in your ma an' John.'

Hal went to rise from the chair when he noticed the door was ajar. 'John, you there? Tell Ma she's wanted.'

He wanted to cry but no tears would come. He wanted to go back to last week when none of this nightmare existed. Last week he was a devil-may-care cowhand carrying out his father's orders. Now he was sitting by his father's deathbed and if he read the signs right he would shortly become responsible for the running of the Big G.

8

'I'm riding into town. Tom Eagan has asked to see me about Pa's estate. I have to go to the bank as well an' sort things out with Thaddeus Farrell.'

'You want as I should come with you, Hal?'

Hal regarded his younger brother for a moment. John had grown into a serious-minded young man. Not turned twenty, he had affected to grow a full beard. Their mother did not approve of men with hair on their faces and let John know her displeasure.

'Well, Ma, it's like this,' he teased her. 'I'm not like Hal here. I can't tell a barefaced lie. So this gives me an out.'

Needless to say Mrs Grant did not appreciate the mirth which this generated in her two sons.

'Sure, John, maybe we'll have time for a drink an' a game of cards down at the Mule's Head.'

A couple of weeks had passed since the death of Harry Grant. He had been interred in the family burial ground located on the Big G ranch.

'Yeah, it'll do us both good to relax a bit. I ain't been in town in a coon's age.'

It was early evening before Hal and John finished the family business. Hal had insisted that John should sit in on the discussions with the family solicitor, Tom Eagan and the bank manager, Thaddeus Farrell.

'John, if something happens to me then you'll have the runnin' of the Big G. At least you'll have a fair idea of how things are. Not like me. I been flung in at the deep end.'

'Hal, you don't think the fellas as hit Pa will try the same with you?' John looked alarmed at the thought.

Hal punched John in the shoulder. 'Just think of it, brother, you'll own everythin'. Won't have to share with me.'

'Don't even joke about it, Hal. If anythin' happens to you . . . Jeez, I don't even want to think about it.'

Hal pulled his brother close and embraced him. 'Brother, I'm gonna be around for a long time.' He held his brother at arm's length. 'We just gotta be vigilant and look out for each other. Pa did warn me.'

When the brothers finished up the family business they sauntered down to their old watering-hole, the Mule's Head.

The first person to greet them was the owner of the establishment, Madam Quigley herself.

'Hal, my dear, am I pleased to see you. Life has been dull since you deserted us.' Madam Quigley was a tall, handsome woman in her late thirties. 'What'll it be, the usual whiskey?'

'Sure, leave us a bottle. This is my brother, John.'

'Hal, do you think I'm in my dotage? I remember John. I was so sorry to hear about your father, Hal. He was a fine man and well-respected in the community. Of course he never came in here. He was too grand for this place.'

Hal leaned confidentially towards the woman. 'You hear anything about who shot Pa?'

For a moment the saloon-owner stared speculatively at Hal then, reaching over, covered his hand with hers. 'Enjoy yourself, you two. I must see to my customers.'

John poured the drinks while Hal stared into the distance.

'You think she knows somethin'?' John asked as he sipped the whiskey. 'Christ, what the hell!' He made a face. 'Does she mix this with cow's piss?'

Hal grinned at his brother. 'That's the trouble with you Grants — born with a silver spoon in your mouth. Don't know how to rough it. When I was your age, boy,' he went on adopting a languid drawl, 'I was drinkin' a couple bottles of this cow's piss every night and still gettin' on ma hoss next mornin' and roundin' up and brandin' a whole herd of cattle. Yes sirree, we was rough an' tough in them good ol' days.'

'Hal, as I live and breathe, if it ain't my old pal come to treat with his old friends.'

A fat man weaved uncertainly before the brothers. His face was flushed from too much liquor. Hal looked up, his own face showing no friendliness.

'Howdy, Jack. Looks like someone been treatin' you to free drinks.'

The fat man dragged a chair across and sat down at their table.

'Hal, I was sure sorry to hear about your pa — bad business, that. If I'd a known he was in town that night I would a stayed by his side. No dirty, murderin' gunman would have gotten anywhere near Harry Grant while Jack Falmouth was on watch.'

Hal said nothing, staring into his glass. Falmouth reached out and gripped the bottle on the table. Without asking permission he put it to his mouth and drank long and deep.

'Aaah, the first drink of the night

always tastes the sweetest,' he exclaimed, keeping a grip on the bottle.

The brothers watched him dispassionately.

'Still the same old Jack, always makin' free with someone else's property,' Hal said at last.

'Hal, now that your pa is dead, rest his soul, I take it you be in charge at the Big G now?'

'That's right, Jack. Smart of you to work that one out.'

Still nursing the whiskey bottle, Falmouth leaned his elbows on the table. 'You won't be forgettin' your old friends then, Hal. I take it you'll be hirin' me as foreman or some such position as befits my experience.'

Hal nodded thoughtfully. 'You know anyone as makes good whiskey, Jack?'

'Huh, why, now you ask, there's a fella up in the Dunlop Hills runs a pretty good still.'

'Well, when you come out to me for the job of foreman bring this fella with you. Tell him he'll have a job for life makin' moonshine for a fat, whiskey-guzzlin', manure-heap that'll be runnin' things at the Big G.' Hal turned to his brother. 'John, make a note to draw up plans for a bakehouse and hire us a baker. We'll need the extra rations to feed fat Jack here when he comes to work for us.'

'Hell, by the time you pay for a whiskey-brewer an' a baker there won't be any left over to pay no wages to no foreman as well,' John countered.

'Ha, ha, ha,' Falmouth chortled. 'You always were one for a joke, Hal.' He took a long, deep drink from the whiskey-bottle. 'When you want me to start?'

'Why, Jack, you can start tonight. Start ridin' as far away from the Big G as you can get.' Hal stared steadily at the fat man.

'Hal, what are you sayin'?' The big man was blinking uncertainly. 'This is Jack Falmouth you're talkin' to. Who stood with you against them there Mortimers on the day they came to

Lourdes to kill your pa and his sidekicks? Why, fearless Jack Falmouth was there right at your side facin' them hellions.'

'If I remember right, on the day the Mortimers came to Lourdes I asked you for help. While the shootin' was goin' on up in the Hot Spur you were hidin' out here in the Mule's Head. You brazened in when you were sure us Grants had finished off the gang. Then a gun went off accidentally an' you shit your britches. Now tell me again that you were a good friend when things got rough.'

'Hal, you got it all wrong. I was out there in the street watchin' your back. I wouldn't have allowed none of them there varmints to sneak up an' backshoot you.'

'John, go get another bottle. Fat Jack here has gone an' finished this one. Unless as Jack will buy us a drink of his own accord?'

'Times are hard, Hal. I'm real down on my luck. That's why I was hopin' you'd give an old friend a start. Tell me you didn't mean all those things you said, Hal. This is me, jolly Jack Falmouth! You can't abandon old friends.'

'Fat Jack, you are a ghost from my misspent youth. Let me warn you, you fat tub of lard, if I come into town again an' you bother me I'll shoot you in the leg so as you can't follow me around. Now, take that bottle you stole off my table an' go and pester some other poor fool. I've had enough of your lyin' and cheatin'.'

The fat man stared with mouth open at the young man. 'You . . . you . . .' he began but got no further.

'Git!'

Jack jumped as the word was barked out at him. There was no mistaking the look in young Hal Grant's eyes. Clutching the whiskey-bottle to his chest the fat man stumbled from the table, a hurt look in his eyes. Hal turned to see John grinning at him.

'You shoulda done that a long time ago, Hal. He's sure one sad old man.'

'I suppose,' Hal sighed. 'He sure soured my evenin'.'

A shadow loomed across the table. Hal looked up to see the saloon-owner regarding him with hands on her generous hips.

'What you do to Jack? He looks as if someone told him his horse had died.'

Hal shrugged but said nothing. The tall woman put her hands on the table and leaned in close.

'I give you three names,' she said in a voice barely above a whisper. 'It never come from me. If you try and claim any such thing I'll deny everything — Scoote, Cambridge and Grey.'

9

'John, I'm leaving you in charge for a while. There's somethin' I promised to do for a fella but with things the way they were I had to put it off. I can't delay any longer.'

'Where you goin', Hal?' There was real concern in John's face. 'Remember what Pa said about watchin' out for those killers. I don't want you comin' home draped over a horse like last time.'

Hal tapped his Colt strapped to his waist, then pointed to the Winchester tucked into his saddle bucket. 'Don't you worry none about me, John. I'm going prepared.' He reached behind and with a slick movement brought out a .38 and showed it to John before replacing it in a small holster attached to his belt.

'Hal, I know you practise regular

with that durn Colt of yours but no matter how fast you are it won't stop a bushwhacker from gettin' you in the back. Pa was hell on wheels with a gun but look what happened to him.'

Hal's eyes turned bleak. 'I know what you're sayin', John, but we can't hide away on the Big G for ever. No bushwhacker is goin' to frighten me into showin' a yellow streak. This trip is just somethin' I gotta do. I been puttin' it off for days. With Pa's funeral outta the way, if I don't do it now I never will.' He turned his head and gazed out towards the horizon. 'It's that fella as I had the run-in with when we rescued the herd. I promised I'd tell his folks what happened to him.'

'Jeez, Hal. What the hell you gonna say? I come to 'pologize, I killed your boy!'

Hal shrugged and walked to his mount. He did not reply till he had swung on board. 'I'll think of somethin', John. It's a goodly ride over to Peterstown. I'll do me a mite of thinkin' on the way.'

John was by his side gripping the bridle and staring up at his brother. 'Take some men with you at least, Hal. Don't go alone into that place.'

'Stop fussin', John, you're like an old maiden aunt.'

John stared after his brother, an uneasy feeling in his stomach. He knew Hal was no slouch with a gun. But then his pa too had been no amateur when it came to shooting. Skill with a gun was no protection against an assassin's bullet from an alleyway or from behind a tree. As John turned away he saw Harvey Baker saddling up but thought nothing of it. Ranch hands came and went all the time on the Big G.

★ ★ ★

Stump Murphy looked at the sweating, dusty cowhand leaning against the bar.

'You're sure he said Peterstown.'

Harvey Baker nodded. 'Sure, Mr Murphy, I just heard the tail end of the talk, but it was Peterstown.'

The big Irishman looked thoughtfully at the cowboy. 'How'd you like to earn yourself fifty dollars?'

'Who do I have to kill?'

Stump Murphy grinned. 'You're my kinda man, Baker. I got three good men to do my killin'. Your job is to take these fellas to the quarry.'

★   ★   ★

It was nudging towards noon before Hal sighted Peterstown. He rode on into the town and stopped at the local saloon. He looked a bit sceptically at the sign over the door. 'The Sheep Dip,' he mused.

As a cowpoke the idea of anything remotely connected with sheep repelled him. However, the ride over had given him a thirst and he needed to ask directions. He pushed inside the swing-doors and walked to the bar. The inmates eyed him with some suspicion. Hal ignored the hard glares directed at him.

'Beer an' information,' he said to the barkeep.

'Beer's a quarter. Information is priceless.' The man behind the bar was a sour-faced individual with balding head.

'I'm after directions. Lookin' for Grand Hill Farm.'

'Follow the trail out west of the town. You'll come to a bridge over the river. Turn right over the bridge an' follow the river for about a mile. You'll come to a right fork. Follow that, about two mile on is the place you're wantin'.'

When Hal left the bar he was unaware of the wave of mirth his exit unleashed.

'Jem, you sumbitch, them directions is to Jennie Fletcher's cathouse. The fella said he wanted Grand Hill Farm — the Hendrons' place.'

The sour-faced man behind the bar smirked across at the speaker. 'You know I hate cowboys after that time they come in my place an' wrecked it. Anyway, that young fella looked as if he needed some relaxation. If he don't like it at Jennie's she'll put him right for the farm.'

They were still laughing some when the four hard-looking men rode up and pushed inside.

'My,' commented Jem, 'Peterstown is sure popular today. Howdy fellas, what's your poison?'

'Whiskey.'

As the barkeep served up, the men looked carefully around the bar. They were tough-looking *hombres* with tied-down, low-slung guns. At no time did their hands stray far from gun butts.

'Jem, you see any cowboys come past here today?' The questioner was a young man with deep-sunk, dark eyes and a hard look on his face.

'Now you say it, a fella left here just ten minutes ago, young fella. He was asking directions.'

'Where was he goin'?'

'Jennie Fletcher's place.'

This brought a burst of mirth from the men sitting at the tables. The bitter young gunman looked angry.

'What the hell's so funny?' he snarled, his hand reaching for his gun.

'Ain't nothing agin' you fellas.' The barman hastily waved his hands in a calming gesture. 'I sent him in the wrong direction is all.'

The gunman turned to the man who looked like one of the cowboys the barman claimed to dislike so much.

'What you think, Harvey? Will he spend some time at the whorehouse?'

Harvey Baker shrugged. 'I'm not sure. He used to hang out a lot at the Mule's Head so he just might stay there a while.'

'Drink up, boys. If we follow him hard to Jennie's we might just catch that cowboy with his britches round his ankles.'

10

Hal eyed the mess of buildings. There was one big, rambling, two-storey timbered house and a clutter of barns and outhouses scattered around the main dwelling. A corral housed about half a dozen horses adjoining another fenced-in area where about two dozen cattle were penned. The whole place bore an air of neglect. Loose shingles were evident and none of the woodwork had seen paint for many seasons. Some of the rails on the fences were hanging loose or missing. Weeds were evident everywhere. Hal frowned.

This was not what he had expected at all. The image he had of Grand Hill Farm was of a single-storey dwelling with chickens pecking around the yard and a vegetable-patch out back with fruit-trees. Certainly the cattle and horses were evidence of some wealth.

Dirt-poor farmers never owned that much stock. And then he had a suspicion that the horses and cattle might be stolen.

Hal shook his head. That couldn't be true, for the boy James had begged Hal not to let on to his mother he was a rustler. It took all his powers of restraint not to ride round the back of the house and examine the brands on the horses and cattle. Instead he dismounted and tied up his horse.

Hal knocked on the front door. The paint was virtually non-existent and the boards had warped, leaving gaps between them. 'Come on in. Don't bother knockin',' a woman's voice called out.

Hal pushed open the door, which was so badly hung it scraped along the floor. He noticed grooves worn on the floorboards where over time the door had been pushed back and forth. Inside was an even greater puzzle.

A bar ran the length of the inner room, behind which a tall elegant woman stood. Her hair was corn-coloured and tied up at the back with a black ribbon. She wore a low-necked silk dress with a string of fat pearls encircling her graceful neck.

'Come on in, cowboy, ain't no one goin' to bite you.'

'Yes, ma'am,' Hal said diffidently, walking up to the bar.

'What'll it be, cowboy — drink, food or women?'

Hal blinked somewhat foolishly. 'Women?' he asked.

'Sure. You want them fat or thin, tall or short, young or old, Injun or black?'

This was all too much for Hal. 'Can I have a drink while I think about it? An' come to think of it I ain't ate anythin' since breakfast. I'll take some of that food on offer.'

'Kate!' the woman bawled out.

After some delay a door at the back of the long room opened and a girl emerged. Hal watched her walk up the room towards them. He caught his breath. A golden mass of hair was piled on top of her head. She had a pale oval face with wide-set eyes the colour of a summer sky. Her lips were full and sensual. Hal could not tell anything about the rest of the girl for her figure was draped in a shapeless pinafore. Without looking at him the girl waited.

'Tell her what you want to eat, cowboy,' the woman behind the bar said, smiling at Hal's obvious bemusement at the sight of the girl.

'Ah . . . I'll have flapjacks and beans if it's no trouble, miss.'

Without a word the girl turned and walked back down the room. In spite of the shapeless dress she wore Hal could see her hips — or imagined he could see her hips sway as she walked. He stared after the vision till she disappeared through the door.

'Well, that's your food sorted. What'll you drink?'

'Ah-huh,' Hal was suddenly back in the room with the woman again. 'Beer, ma'am.'

'She makes the flapjacks fresh,' the

woman said as she handed him his beer. 'So it'll be a while before she brings your meal.'

Hal nodded and sipped slowly. He was completely bewildered. How was he to broach the subject of the woman's son? This so-called Grand Hill Farm was nothing more than a bawdy-house. Maybe he should just have his drink, eat his meal and ride on out again.

'Come far, cowboy?'

Before he could reply the sound of horses approaching brought the woman's head round. She walked to a window and peered out through the dirty glass. 'Consarn it, we usually get no one during the daytime and now here's another bunch of fellas arriving.' She patted her hair and walked back to the bar and awaited the new arrivals.

In a while the door-bottom grated along the floor again. Hal glanced up as a couple of men entered. Though he did not show any outward signs he became somewhat wary. He had seen men like this before. Mean-eyed and with pistols strapped low on their thighs. The handles of Bowie knives protruded from leather sheaths. One of the men was of blocky build with a round, washed-out face. The youngest of the pair was a surly-looking youth with deep-sunk, dark eyes. Hal sipped at his beer and watched and waited.

'Howdy, fellas, wasn't expectin' any punters till later. What's the matter, you got ants in your pants?'

'Hell, Jennie, less of the jawin' and put us up a bottle.'

Hal noticed some tables set back against the far wall and decided to park himself there, away from the two newcomers. He drifted in that direction.

'What's the matter, cowboy, you don't like our company?'

Hal did not stop walking. He reached the table and set down his beer. While moving across the room he had slipped the rawhide thong that held his Colt safe while riding. He was able to do this as his body shielded the movement of his free hand.

'I asked you a question, cowboy. Don't you know when a fella asks a question he expects an answer? Seems to me you got the manners of a hog.'

Hal turned fully and faced the two men. They had both braced themselves against the bar and had edged well apart. He knew by the set of their faces and the way the men rested their hands on their gun butts that they wanted trouble. No matter what he said or did they would push and push till he either backed down or made a play.

'Listen here, Billy Cambridge, I want no trouble. This fella's gonna drink his beer and ride on outta here.' The brothel-keeper was looking over at Hal with a pleading look in her eyes. 'Isn't that right, fella?'

Hal didn't look at the woman. He kept his eyes on the younger of the gunmen, sensing he was the more dangerous. The image of Madam Quigley was surfacing in his mind. *I'll give you three names*, she had said — *Scoote, Cambridge and Grey*.

It was becoming clear that this was no chance meeting. If Madam Quigley was correct, Hal now was confronted with the men who had murdered his father. Somehow they had tracked him down and were setting him up for a killing. Anger was beginning to grow in him. Hal tried to keep calm. He was in a dangerous situation and only his skill with his Colt would save him.

'Billy Cambridge,' he mused, 'now where have I heard that name before? That fella with you, his name Grey by any chance?'

The men at the bar blinked and looked momentarily puzzled. 'What the hell, cowboy, you trying to be smart? What about our names, anyways?'

'I was told about three rats that went around backshootin' people. The names of Cambridge, Grey an' Scoote were given me. I was gonna come lookin' for you yellow-bellies but it looks as if I don't need look no further.'

The men slid sideways glances at each other. This wasn't right. They had been told the man they were to kill was a milksop youngster more interested in drinking and whoring than in fighting. They had looked forward to taunting the cowboy and scaring him some before shooting him. This fella stood facing them, apparently unafraid and almost daring them to make their play. It was he who was doing the taunting. It made them nervous. This wasn't how it should be. The tension in the room grew. Even the woman behind the bar was afraid to intervene in case she sparked off something.

Then the door to the kitchen squeaked open and the blonde girl backed out with a tray of food for Hal. So wound up were the gunmen the interruption pushed them over the edge and they went for their shooters. As his brother John had observed, Hal practised daily with his Colt. His draw was slick and fast.

The room exploded in noise and flying lead. Hal did not flinch as bullets spun past his body. He triggered his own pistol with cool, calm deliberation. His first choice was Cambridge. Hal's shots were true and the young gunman was hurled back against the bar. He was still triggering his pistol as he slid to the floor. The second man went down twisting away from Hal as if trying to make a smaller target. He pitched to the floor. Suddenly the thunderous noise ended and the room was filled with blue gunsmoke and the smell of cordite. Two bodies lay in the sawdust, crimson stains spreading over the floor.

11

There was a sudden crash behind Hal. He spun round, his hand snaking for his second pistol, tucked into the back of his belt. He glimpsed the flaxen-haired girl staring at the dead bodies on the floor of the bar. At her feet lay the tray of food meant for him. As he turned a shot blasted in from the vicinity of the window. He felt a glancing blow on his left arm and dropped to one knee. The spare pistol was in his right hand and in spite of the sudden pain in his arm he was still able to trigger bullets towards the window. Glass had cascaded into the room with the shot from outside and Hal now blasted the remainder of the glass to smithereens as he tried to hit the gunman shooting into the bar.

No further shots came in. Then Hal's trigger clicked on a used cartridge.

Now he had two empty pistols. Hastily he began to reload when he noticed the blood pouring down his arm. It was only then he realized he had been hit by the ambusher on the outside of the building. Then he paused in his task as he heard the hoof-beats. He listened as the noise of the fleeing horseman faded into the distance. He stood and looked around the room.

The men he had shot lay motionless in their own blood, their guns lying useless beside them. Behind the bar the woman was holding her hand to her mouth and staring at him with some apprehension. The young girl who had dropped the food-tray was also gazing at him with the same trepidation as she would look at a dangerous animal suddenly let loose in the barroom.

Hal looked at the spilled food at the girl's feet. Before he could say anything there was a sudden rush of movement within the building. Doors slammed, footsteps were heard and voices calling. Feet clattered on the stairs and gradually the room filled with females of varying ages, wearing long, colourful wrap-around gowns that entirely covered their persons. Behind the women came a young man in shirt and britches. He was broad in the shoulder and looked as bewildered as the females.

Without exception they stopped and stared wide-eyed at the bodies sprawled in the sawdust.

'Oh my God!'

'Laws a mercy!'

'What on earth!'

The room was filled with fluttering female forms. Hal retreated to the table on which he had rested his beer before being sucked into combat with his father's murderers.

'Dad bang,' the young man said. He stuck his thumbs behind his braces and stared with some consternation at the scene of carnage in his mistress's barroom.

'There's the fella what did it.' Jennie Fletcher said. She raised a large glass of whiskey to her mouth and drained it off without pause.

By now everyone had turned to stare at the young man standing by the tables, awkwardly reloading his weapons. Blood was running from the wound in his upper arm down on to the back of his hand. A hush fell as the roomful of females stared at him.

'Kate,' the saloon owner called out again. 'That young fella's hurt. Take him in back and bind up his wound. Jim, you get rid of them there bodies.'

The young man in shirt and britches looked worried. 'What do I do with them, Miss Jennie?'

'Drag them out in a field somewheres. Then get a shovel an' bury them.' She poured herself another large whiskey.

'You'd better come with me,' the flaxen-haired young girl told Hal.

By now Hal had reloaded his spare pistol. He pushed it into his holster. It had been a tricky job with his wounded arm throbbing and painful with every movement. The spare pistol he thrust back into its hiding place. He felt safe now with both weapons loaded. The hoof-beats he had heard indicated the rest of the gang had fled.

The girl was staring at the blood on his hand. It dripped on to the floor — the bright-red blobs quickly absorbed into the sawdust. Her face was pale and she was biting at her lower lip.

'I guess I should bind it up and stop spreadin' blood around the place,' Hal offered.

She led the way towards the back. Around them the girls parted and stared curiously at Hal.

'Howdy, cowboy. When Kate patches you up you come right back. We'll take care of any other aches you might have,' one of them called.

'Sure thing, cowboy, a big handsome fella like you, I'd do it for free.'

There was a chorus of laughter and more banter as the girls found a way to allay their fright. The suddenness of the violence had jolted them out of a quiet day's rest. Hal was grateful when the door closed behind him and he was alone with the girl.

'I'm sorry I frighted you out there,' he said lamely.

She was busy pouring hot water into a basin from a kettle on the stove. 'Sit over there.' She indicated a canebottomed chair that had seen better days. 'Do you want to take your shirt off or will I cut the sleeve?'

'I'd better take the shirt off. It's the only one I got till I get back home.'

'You're not from around here?' she asked, placing a wad of cotton cloth in the basin. She suddenly noticed his awkwardness as he tried to unbutton his shirt. 'Here, let me help.' Her fingers were slim and nimble as she worked on the buttons. Hal stared at the head of golden hair inclined towards him. He wanted to bury his nose in the soft golden tresses and sniff them up into him. The faint scent of herbs tickled his nostrils. It took all his self-control not to reach out and pull her to him.

She helped him shed his shirt. In the process of observing her he had forgotten about the wound in his side that was covered in cotton pads.

'You seem to be collecting wounds. Obviously a gunman's trade is a dangerous occupation.' She was working on his arm by now.

'Gunman? I ain't no gunman, miss. Those fellas were the ones as killed my pa. They were aiming to kill me too. I ain't no gunslinger.'

She said nothing but concentrated on cleaning the wound in his arm.

'I'm not a doctor but it looks as if the bullet went straight through. Can you work your arm?'

He flexed his arm and except for the pain of the wound in his muscle he could feel no restriction in the movement.

'I reckon.'

'You'd better get a doctor to see to that as soon as you can. I'll bind it up for now. That'll stop the blood and then I'll make you a sling to keep it rested.'

In a short time he was bandaged and back in his shirt.

'Thank you, miss. I gotta go an' see Jennie out in the bar. I have some bad news for her.'

The girl turned back to the stove, already dismissing him as she worked at the pots.

'Tell me, is Jennie her working name? I mean is that for the men as come here?'

She turned those disturbing blue eyes on him. 'That's her name, Jennie Fletcher.'

He pondered this for a moment. 'What happened to Mrs Hendron? I was directed here from Peterstown when I asked for directions to Grand Hill Farm.'

She looked faintly amused. 'This is Jennie Fletcher's sporting-house. Grand Hill is five or six mile further on the other side of the river.'

12

Ronald Preston paced impatiently up and down at the railroad depot. His resentment was evident in the scowl on his face. It was a face that never showed a smile even when things were going right. From time to time he pulled out a watch and studied it as if he could not believe it was running true. He would shove the timepiece back in his pocket and start pacing again. Minutes later he would take out the watch and go through the same procedure of studying the position of the hands and then pushing it impatiently back into his pocket.

Preston was straw-boss of Stump Murphy's ranch, the Lazy M. He was a big, loose-boned man with a long narrow face. Deep pouches beneath his eyes added to his demeanour of sour vindictiveness. He awaited the arrival of the train with barely suppressed irritation. The train was not late by any means, but was running on time. It was Preston's impatience that was causing his annoyance.

He hated being away from the Lazy M, for he believed his ranch hands were, without exception, slothful layabouts who would slack off as soon as his vigilant eye was taken off them. Only a summons from his boss could have resulted in his leaving the iron-rod supervision of his hired hands.

'Meet the noon train. I got some men comin' in on that train. Bring them back here,' Murphy had told him.

'What the hell we want more hands for? Unless you want to get rid of some of the good-for-nothin' layabouts you got workin' for you already.'

Murphy looked at his ranch manager and grinned crookedly. 'These ain't no ranch hands, at least that's not what I'm hirin' them for. So keep your measly eyes off them. These men are special. They are the first wave of a new task-force I'm assemblin'. The Wyomin' Ranchers' Institute has come round to my way of thinkin' and is hirin' some troubleshooters.'

Preston's eyes widened. 'They've agreed to take action against the sodbusters?'

Murphy's broad lips thinned out as he smiled at his foreman. 'Strange how the institute came round to my way of thinkin' after that unfortunate accident to Harry Grant. It was sure fortuitous, that. There won't be any more trouble from that quarter now his idle, good-for-nothin' son is in charge of the Big G. Sure hope nothin' happens to young Hal Grant. It'd be a real tragedy for that family.'

When Preston left on his way to meet the train he looked with some curiosity at the man tying up his horse outside. His face was covered in blood. The foreman figured he looked as if he had put his head through a window, with all the small cuts on his face.

For Stump Murphy the sight of Dick

Scoote with a blood-spattered face brought him a distinct feeling of unease. With an imperceptible nod to the man he wandered into his back office.

'What the hell happened to you an' where's Cambridge and Grey.'

'They're dead,' the gunman said wearily, slumping down on to a chair. 'That goddamn cowboy shot them both. He gunned them down before I could get a bead on him. They were intendin' to keep him occupied so as I could put a bullet in him from outside. Then all hell broke loose an' when I looked in the window Billy an' Doug vere lyin' in the floor all shot to pieces. I put a slug in that there cowboy but he turned round quicker than a riled-up rattler an' almost blew my goddamn head off. I lammed outta there quicker than a coyote with hound-dogs on his trail.'

'Jesus H. Christ!' Murphy ground out. 'Of all the luck! Did he get a look at you?'

'Nah, I was outside in the yard. He was inside at the bar.'

'Where'd you catch up with him, anyways?'

'Jennie Fletcher's sportin'-house. We was gonna have us some fun with the girls after we killed that there cowboy.'

A slow thoughtful smile grew on the big Irishman's face. 'Jennie's place? So that's where he goes for his fun. Her name's on that list.'

'What, Jennie?' Scoote looked surprised. 'What the hell's she done?'

Instead of answering directly, Murphy asked a question of the killer. 'You see any cattle about her place?'

Scoote pursed his lips for a moment. 'Come to think of it there were some beeves out back.'

'Stolen beeves, no doubt. If a damn sodbuster wants to stray from his frumpy old wife, he goes out an' steals himself a steer. He drives it to Jennie and instead of money he pays with our cattle. Has himself a rattlin' good time at our expense. We warned Jennie to stop takin' in stolen beeves. Seems as if she ignored our warnin'.' He eyed the bloody face before him. 'Go an' get cleaned up an' then make yourself ready. There's a bunch of men coming in on the noon train. As soon as they're fed and watered I want you to guide them back out to Jennie Fletcher's place. Them fellas might just want a bit of fun after their journey.' He frowned suddenly. 'You say Grant gunned down Cambridge and Grey? Them two were old hands at the killin' game. He must have caught them off guard. Where's Grant at now?'

'I guess he's still out there.'

'An' where's Baker?'

'He's gone back to the Big G to find out what he can.'

'Did Grant see him?'

'Nah, Baker lay out in the woods while we went after Grant.'

Murphy nodded. 'Good.'

★ ★ ★

Way back up the track the train hooted its salutation to the town to let everyone know it was arriving at the depot. With clouds of steam and screeching brakes it rolled to a stop at the Lourdes depot. Ronald Preston put away his watch and waited for the disembarking to begin.

The guard called out the name of the station for the benefit of those who might have been unaware of their whereabouts. Doors were opening and the foreman of the Lazy M watched with some anticipation for the men who had come to Lundon County to help clear out the rustlers and solve the cattle-stealing that plagued the big ranchers. Momentarily he wondered how he would know these men. As they stepped down from the carriages he was in no doubt any more.

They wore slouch-hats and long dusters that brushed against the heels of polished boots. Each man carried a rifle and a shotgun. Beneath the coats crossed gun belts could be seen. The

men walked up the train towards
Ronald Preston and he felt a little
shiver of apprehension as he watched
them approach.

13

Hal stood nursing his beer while he pondered his next move. During the short time he had been in the kitchen with the girl the bodies of the gunmen had been dragged outside. The girls huddled together, discussing the events and eyeing up the young cowboy. After a few half-hearted attempts to engage him with their charms they had left him to his own devices.

'It true what you said about them fellas killin' your pa?' Jennie asked.

Hal nodded wearily. 'Yeah. I was given three names, Cambridge, Grey and Scoote. At least that's two of them that'll do no more bushwhackin'. I guess the fella as shot me from the window was Scoote. I reckon after Pa I was next on their list.'

'What's your name, cowboy? I guess I ought to know who it is that's killing off my customers.'

'Name's Hal Grant, I'm from the Big G on the south side of Lourdes.' Hal didn't think it prudent to tell the woman that since the death of his father he now owned the biggest spread in the county. 'I sure am sorry to bring this trouble on you, Miss Jennie. The barkeep in Peterstown directed me to this place when I asked directions to Grand Hill Farm. I reckon I ought to pay him a visit and find out why the son of a bitch sent me here. My guess is he was in with those killers. I was sent out here so as them three killers would know where to find me.'

The kitchen door swung open and the girl appeared with another tray of food. Hal looked towards her and then turned back to the brothel-keeper.

'There's my supper. It's too late to ride on out to Grand Hill now. I guess I would either miss the place altogether or arrive in the middle of the night. Do you have a bed I could rent? An' I'll pay for any damage you suffered.'

Jennie Fletcher smiled wryly. 'Is that

a room with company?'

By now the girl was by Hal's side with the food-tray.

'This little filly will do just fine.' Hal grinned invitingly at the girl.

Without looking at Hal the girl set the tray carefully on the counter. With her hands now empty she stepped back a pace and slapped Hal hard across the face. So forceful was the clout that Hal's head was jerked sideways. The blow was so unexpected and sudden Hal was caught out. With gaping mouth he turned to remonstrate with his attacker but she was halfway back to the kitchen.

'What the hell . . . ?' Hal ruefully rubbed his stinging face. 'What'd I say?' He heard a chuckle behind him.

'That's our Kate,' the saloon-owner told him. 'Now what were you sayin' about company?'

Still rubbing his cheek Hal turned back and stared at the food. 'I guess I'll sleep on my lonesome tonight.' He picked up the tray and walked across to the tables, pondering the strange behaviour of the female kind.

By the time he had finished his meal customers were arriving and the place was filling up with a motley collection of farm-labourers and cowpunchers. Hal went out to see to his pony. Just as he was wondering where to stable her, the helper Jim came in from the fields, covered in dirt. He looked warily at Hal.

'Just buried those two fellas you shot,' he volunteered. Then, noticing Hal with his pony, he asked. 'You riding on?'

'Nah, I reckon on havin' myself a good night's sleep an' then make an early start in the mornin'. Where can I bed down my pony?'

'I'll look after her for you.' The youngster reached for the reins. 'You picked a girl for yourself yet?'

'I said I needed a good night's sleep. I'll be sleepin' alone.' Hal rubbed his cheek thoughtfully, remembering the stinging rebuke from the blonde Kate and wondering what he had done wrong.

Jim grinned happily. 'You won't get no sleep tonight less you is a sound sleeper. Place is fillin' up. They'll be at it most of the night. Place'll be bedlam till the small hours.'

Hal looked suitably dismayed. 'What's a fella to do?' he said dolefully. 'I sure could do with some sleep. This arm's hurtin' like hell. I figure to do a heap of ridin' tomorrow.' The next day he expected to finish his errand of mercy and then start back to the Big G.

'You take my advice,' the youngster indicated with his head. 'Sleep in the barn. There's plenty of straw to make a soft bed. You won't be disturbed there.'

Hal's eyebrows lifted in appreciation. He fished a dollar from his pocket. 'Catch.' He tossed the coin to the boy.

Jim's eyes widened. 'Thanks, mister. What time you want waked in the mornin'?'

Hal was grateful he had taken Jim's advice. The straw was warm and comfortable. He could hear nothing of the revelry from the house. Even so sleep was a long time coming.

His mind would not rest as it alternated between the gunfight in the bar and the blonde girl who had hit him. By the time he fell asleep he still hadn't figured what he had said or done to provoke the slap.

When sleep came he dreamed of a blonde girl who was using a large frying-pan to batter him around the head and face. As he rolled about, endeavouring to dodge the blows, at the same time he was trying to ask the girl why she was hitting him. Before she could answer she changed into the dour Cambridge. His face was transformed into a leering skull and instead of a frying-pan he held a large pistol. 'I killed your pa, and now it's your turn,' the skull mouthed and a finger pulled the trigger.

The gunshots were loud and real and clear. Hal jolted upright from the straw. He was trembling as he glared round him wildly. In his hand was the Colt that had blasted two men into a burial place in a field by a bawdy-house. He was bathed in sweat and he shook his head to clear it but the gunshots continued. It took moments for Hal to register he wasn't dreaming. The gunshots were real and coming from next door.

14

Kate Prentice jerked as the shots rang out. She had prepared a batch of sourdough and had walked into the pantry to place them on a shelf to cool off. The original inhabitants of the house had built a stone pantry which no matter the temperature outside, remained cool day or night. Kate heard the screams and the shots. She was about to rush out into the house when she paused. Listening to the sounds coming from the bawdy-house she began to think she would be safer staying where she was.

She had worked late preparing food and then cleaning up after the cooking. The thought of walking back home so late in the evening never bothered Kate. She carried an old worn-out pistol that her father, when he was alive, had taught her to use. In her eighteen years she had never had occasion to pull out the gun, never mind use it to protect herself. Though she would not admit it something else had held her back from leaving for home.

The young cowboy involved in the shoot-out had intrigued her. Jennie and she had discussed his tale of his father's murder. Originally she had dismissed him as just another gunfighter. After talking to Jennie she began to believe she had misjudged him. They figured he had been forced into defending himself.

His assumption that she was a dove still rankled. On thinking over her action after she had hit him she regretted only one thing. She should have used a clenched fist to hit him instead of the flat of her hand. The thought amused her greatly as she worked. Still, when he took his shirt off for her to administer to his injured arm it had made her heart beat a little faster. She had kept her head bowed so he would not notice the expression in her eyes as she washed the wound and bandaged it.

Now once more Jennie Fletcher's bordello was rocked by gunfire.

* * *

Hal had slept in his clothes, removing only his boots and gun-belt before bedding down. Quickly he retrieved his boots and strapped on his guns. His wounded arm was stiff and sore but he ignored the discomfort. Within minutes of being so abruptly awakened Hal was peering out into the yard.

Half a dozen horses were tied to the hitching-rail. A dark figure stood on the porch. Hal could see that the man was holding a rifle.

By now the gunshots had ceased, to be replaced by screams from inside the house. Hal guessed whoever was doing the shooting had left a man to guard the horses. Quickly he ran to the rear of the barn. It took a few moments to find rotten boards and kick a hole in the rear wall. Quickly he slid out into the night.

Unobserved by the guard he crouched by the corner of the house. For a moment he was undecided what to do. Then he holstered his Colt and drew out his Bowie. For a moment he gathered himself, then he was running silently for the house. Then he was on the porch and launching himself at the lonely sentinel.

At the same time as Hal went for the man a high-pitched scream echoed inside. The guard half-turned towards the door as if in two minds whether to enter. He never got the chance to make up his mind. Hal drove the honed blade into the man's spine and at the same time slammed him against the wall of the house.

He could feel the spasms of the guard as his spine was severed. Hal heaved hard upwards. The knife blade tore up inside the man, severing nerves and tendons. Twitching in his death-throes the man slid slowly down the wall, whimpering softly as he died.

As Hal retrieved his knife and wiped the blade on the man's coat there were more cries and screams from inside the house. As he sheathed the Bowie he noted the garment the dead man was wearing was a long duster-coat. Quickly Hal stripped the body and donned the duster. The weapon Hal had assumed to be a rifle he discovered now was a shotgun. That he took also. The man's slouch-hat completed the disguise. As he straightened up the door beside him opened. A broad swath of light fell across the patio. Hal turned the shotgun towards the opening.

'You wanna come inside, Larson? The boys are fixin' to have some fun with the doves.'

Keeping the shotgun aimed at the door Hal grunted. 'Sure.' He moved to the opening. He could feel the weight of shotgun cartridges in the duster's pocket.

★　★　★

The screams and gunfire going on in the house was unnerving. Kate fumbled in her bag for the ancient pistol. Now she dug it out and examined the loads. Old though it might be, it was still fully functional for Kate kept it oiled and serviceable. The weapon was heavy and awkward and she had to use both hands to hold and fire it. Then she heard the kitchen door crash open.

Footsteps entered the room. Kate kept very still. She also kept the pistol pointed at the door of the larder that led into the kitchen.

'Nobody here,' a man's rough voice called out.

The footsteps retreated. The horrendous noise of men and women being butchered continued. Kate pushed the door to her den open and, crouching down, crept across the kitchen floor. The man who had burst inside had left the door ajar. Kate edged her head around the opening and stared into a scene from hell.

She could see men standing around

the barroom. They looked huge in duster-coats and slouch-hats. All were heavily armed. Two bodies lay on the floor weeping blood into the sawdust. Kate's eyes were wide with terror. Then she saw Jennie.

The bordello-owner was sitting on a chair. She was slumped forward. Her dress was ripped and the string of pearls had disappeared from round her neck. Blood wept from a cut in her eyebrow and a crimson rivulet streaked down her face.

Footsteps clattered on the stairway. Weeping girls stumbled into the room followed by more duster-coated men. The girls were clutching robes to cover themselves. They huddled together like older versions of frightened children. In fact some were no more than children.

'That's all from upstairs.'

The room was crowded with men and girls now.

A big, lean man with a neat moustache and bushy eyebrows called out: 'Tell Larson he can come inside now. It looks as if we've got everyone.'

Another of the dreadful men stepped inside. He had a shotgun in his hands pointed loosely into the room. His hat was pulled down low so that his face was obscured. Kate shrank lower on to the floor. She wondered what horror was coming next. The hand that held her ancient weapon was sweating. When she looked down she could see her hand shaking. She realized her whole body was trembling.

15

'Barney, you used to be a barkeep. Get behind that there bar and start servin'. I'll have bourbon.'

A man with an untidy moustache grinned at the big man and obediently edged behind the bar. He began placing glasses and bottles on the counter.

'Any you fellas want to take these whores upstairs for a little sport while I hold court down here is welcome.'

There were a few sniggers and some of the men started forward. They did not ask the girls. Just jerked the female of their choice from among the terrified women and cuffed them towards the stairway. Three men disappeared upstairs, leaving four men in the room including the guard invited in from outside. The remaining girls huddled together. They made little whimpering noises like young puppies separated from their mother.

The leader took a swig of bourbon and made a face. 'Cheap booze you serve here, ma'am,' he commented, looking with contempt at the woman slumped before him. He jerked his head to one of the men. 'Scoote, ask her about the cowboy.'

Dick Scoote stepped forward, a malicious grin on his face. The cuts on his face gave him a fierce and sinister look. 'Where did Grant go, Jennie?'

Jennie looked at him with dull eyes. 'The cowboy, ain't he upstairs? He paid for a room.'

One of the men with a whiskey-glass in his hand chortled. 'If that's the case he's dead now. We killed every son-abitch up there. Except for the women that is.'

'Well, that's one problem solved, anyways,' the leader surmised.

In the kitchen the girl felt a stab of anger. She stared with some hatred at the men so casually talking of killing men at play. Without thinking she raised the pistol and aimed it into the room but could not bring herself to fire.

The leader reached inside his coat, took a folded paper from his inside pocket and spread it on the bar-top.

'This here is a list of all rustlers in the territory, Jennie Fletcher. Your name is on this list as one of the guilty.'

The woman stared up at the man. 'I never rustled a steer in my life,' she said uncertainly. 'I hardly know one end of a steer from the other.'

'Maybe not personally, Jennie,' crowed Scoote. 'But you sure took stolen cattle in payment for your services. You can't deny that.'

Jennie blinked at her accuser, unsure how to reply to this.

'As a consequence of your criminal activities,' the leader of the raiders went on, 'we pronounce you guilty an' we intend to take you out to the barn an' hang you.'

Jennie stared aghast at the words. 'Hang me — you can't hang me. Only the law can do that.'

The big man laughed. 'We are the

law. We been appointed by the Institute of Wyoming Ranchers to dispense justice throughout Lundon County. Have you any last requests?' The man turned to his barkeep. 'Pour me some more of that godawful bourbon, Barney.'

'What about my girls — what will happen to them?' Jennie asked in a scared voice.

The leader of the gang leered at the saloon-keeper. 'They'll be all right. They'll like as not keep you company, hangin' about in the barn.'

This brought sniggers from his companions.

Jennie Fletcher stared aghast at the man. 'You're not . . . you don't mean to hang everyone!'

'My instructions was to put this place out of business. To do that we mean to kill every livin' thing here an' burn the buildin' to the ground. We don't want nobody to start up again now, do we?'

'You can't do this.' Jennie's face was stricken. 'Hang me if you must but leave my girls alone. With me gone they'll move on somewhere else.'

The man turned and handed his glass to the barkeep for a refill.

'I . . . got money I saved up,' Jennie said with a note of desperation in her voice. 'It's all yours. You take it and let us go free. We'll go away. Leave the county and never come back.'

She had caught the big man's attention. He turned from the bar, his glass now filled again with amber liquor.

'Money you say? Dollars?'

'Yes, I was savin' it against my old age.'

'Where is this money? Is it in a bank or where?'

Jennie shook her head vigorously. 'It's here, right here. I don't trust no bank.'

'OK, let's see this loot then. I don't trust no whorehouse-keeper, neither.' He tossed back the drink and waited.

'First your promise to let us go.'

'All right, you have my word. You an' your whores won't have any worry from us when we get our hands on that there brass.'

Jenny slumped in her chair. 'Thank

God and his holy saints,' she muttered, 'thank God. It's behind the bar under some loose boards.'

'Go get it then.'

Jennie rose from her chair and walked round to the back of the bar. The grinning barkeep pushed past her and came out into the room. Jennie's head disappeared behind the bar and could be heard rummaging about. Her head reappeared again. She leaned forward her hands hidden beneath the bar.

'You promise, you'll let us all go on our way.'

'Sure, you are all goin' one way — to hell.' And the big man with the bushy eyebrows laughed harshly.

Jennie brought up the object she had been holding. It was a double-action pepperbox English revolver. She was holding it with both hands and pointing it at the man. 'Why don't you show me the way?' she said as she pulled the trigger.

The grin on his face vanished and he

flung himself to the floor. He was fast but he still took a slug in the shoulder. His companion, the one who had served as barkeep, was bringing up his Colt when the man in the duster by the doorway strode swiftly forward and clouted him on the back of the head with his shotgun. He went down without a sound. The shotgun moved to cover the leader as he pulled his shooter from leather.

''Less you want me to finish what Jennie started just drop that there weapon.'

The man stopped and let the gun drop to the sawdust. He stared balefully at Hal. 'You ain't Larson.'

Out of the corner of his eye the cowboy was watching Scoote. Thinking he was unobserved the bushwhacker was going for his gun. Hal didn't hesitate. He turned the shotgun and, aiming low, pulled the trigger. The shotgun blast was shockingly loud in the enclosed space. It took Scoote in the leg and flung him off balance. He fell to the floor screaming and grabbing a ruined leg.

Hal looked up towards the bar. Jennie Fletcher was staring at him in disbelief.

'Cowboy, you sure turn up in the most unexpected places.'

Hal grinned crookedly at her. 'I'll say this much. You got guts. That was a helluva stunt pullin' that pepperbox.'

Her grin was equally crooked as she replied: 'You don't run a sporting-house as long as I have without learning a few survival tricks.'

Scoote was lying on the floor groaning in agony. Around him a red stain was growing in the sawdust. Hal kicked the wounded leader in the side.

'Shed your hardware an' then get over there an' tend to your hired bushwhacker afore he bleeds to death.'

'Damn you, can't you see I'm wounded myself?'

'A bullet in the shoulder never killed anyone, 'less you die of gangrene.'

With hate-filled eyes the man pulled

out his Colt and dropped it in the sawdust. Holding his injured shoulder he rose to his feet and walked over to Scoote. 'What the hell am I supposed to do now?' he snarled.

'He's your hound-dog, you look to him.' Hal replied callously. He heard the footsteps on the stairs and whirled bringing up the shotgun. A gunnie, minus his duster was on the stairway, a Colt in his hand.

'It's all right,' Hal called keeping his face hidden with the brim of his hat. 'The woman cut loose with a hideout gun. We got her now. Tell the rest of the boys to come on down. We gotta clear out now.'

'Kill the sonabitch! That ain't Larson!'

16

The gunman on the stairs reacted quickly. He snapped off a shot at Hal. Perhaps because he was still on the stairs he shot high. Something stirred Hal's hair and his borrowed slouch-hat was snatched from his head. Hal was bringing up the shotgun. He had not reloaded. There was only one barrel left. The man was triggering another shot. Hal did not know where that one went — by then he had fired the remaining barrel.

The blast caught the man midsection. He screamed and folded over. As he grabbed his stomach crimson spurted from between his fingers.

Hal caught the movement of the man on the floor beside Scoote. There was the glint of light on the barrel of a gun as the man snatched up Scoote's discarded weapon.

There was a wicked glint of triumph in his face as he aimed the Colt. 'Die cowboy, your time has come.'

Hal was caught out. The shotgun was empty. By the time he dropped it and went for his Colt the man on the floor would have triggered off a couple of shots. The wounded man was relishing his triumph. Even though Jennie Fletcher was armed she was stuck behind the bar and unsighted. Hal tensed, ready to hurl the shotgun and chance a fast draw. He figured he might have a chance of killing his opponent even as he was downed. He saw a figure walking in from the kitchen. His eyes flickered sideways. The gunman noted the glance.

'Don't try to fox me, cowboy. We killed everyone down here.'

'You missed me,' the blonde-hired girl from the kitchen said.

That was when the man swung round and triggered a shot towards the voice. Kate flinched but pulled the trigger of her old pistol. The shot hit the groaning

Scoote in the side of the head and killed him. Hal's shotgun hit the floor. He plucked his Colt from the holster and fired, low and accurate.

Kate was pulling at the trigger and bullets were hitting all around the fallen men. It was Hal's shots that entered the leader's neck and chest, punching him sideways on to his dead companion. The raider's Colt discharged into the floor and he was still.

Hal could hear the clicking of Kate's pistol as she stood with her weapon at arm's length, pulling the trigger on to empty cartridges. Quickly he strode over to the girl and put a hand on to the weapon. He could feel the pistol trembling in her grip. 'It's over now, miss.'

She turned frightened eyes on him and stared at him wonderingly. 'You're alive.'

He looked back into those startlingly blue eyes and smiled ruefully. 'Sorry to disappoint you, Miss Kate, someone sure as hell's been tryin' awful hard lately to kill me.'

The clatter of feet on the floor above broke the little intimacy between them. Hal spun round expecting to see more gunmen on the stairs. Not sure of how many rounds he had left in his pistol he lunged for the Colt that the leader of the raiders had discarded. On one knee he awaited developments. There were shouts from upstairs and then comparative silence. Hal waited, tense and watchful.

'Looks like they holed up in the upper floor,' he called to the saloon-keeper. 'We'll have to smoke them out.'

Cautiously he went to the stairs, expecting at any moment to come under fire.

'Your friends are all dead down here,' he yelled. 'If you don't want the same thing to happen to you then do as I say. Throw your weapons down the stairs an' come down backwards with your hands behind your heads.'

He waited in silence. There was a sudden commotion outside and he heard men yelling — then the sound of hoof-beats.

'They've gone out the back windows,' Jennie yelled.

Hal rushed to the front entrance. With the door slightly ajar he peered outside. He could hear horses running in the distance. For a few moments he watched and waited but in the end he concluded Jennie was right and the men had escaped.

When he turned back into the room he saw the raider he had hit sitting up with his hands to his head. The man was staring at his boss and Scoote, lying in their own blood. When he turned Hal was looming over him.

'Howdy, Barney, it looks as if you're all that's left of Quantrill's raiders.'

'Huh?' The man stared blankly up at Hal. 'What's goin' on an' who the hell are you?'

The borrowed Colt hung loose in Hal's hand. 'I want to know who hired you for this job?'

'Go to hell, I ain't tellin' you nothin'.'

Hal could hear Jennie calling up the stairs to the girls who had been dragged up by the raiders. He turned to watch them trailing down into the barroom, frightened and tearful. Jennie was trying to comfort them. She went behind the bar and set out drinks.

'What about you, cowboy?' she called. 'Drinks are on the house.'

'No thanks, I could sure use a coffee — strong and black.'

'That's Kate's department.'

Hal looked at the blonde girl. After all that had happened she looked pale but composed. She smiled wanly at him.

'Sure, do you want anything to eat?'

'Biscuits and eggs would be good.'

'I got some fresh bread I made last night before the . . . before this happened.'

When the girl disappeared into the kitchen Hal turned his attention to the captive.

'I was hopin' this son of a bitch could tell us who is behind this raid. He's decided not to oblige,' he said to Jennie.

'Best thing is to hang him,' she returned. Jennie was busy serving drinks to her girls as well as supping bourbon from a well-filled glass. 'That's what they were fixin' to do to us.'

'That's a damn good idea. Ask Jim to help me. We'll take him out the barn and throw a rope over a rafter.'

For the first time the man looked worried. 'You can't hang me.' Instinctively his hand strayed to his neck and he began to finger it as if he could already feel the noose.

'Jim's dead,' one of the girls said tonelessly. 'Those goddamn bastards shot him. They shot Horse Kearney and Joe Poison and Jack Talbot — all lying up there shot to hell.'

Hal turned to the captive. His eyes were icy cold. 'Jim was just a boy. I guess I'll have to hang you by myself. Get me a rope,' he called. 'I need to tie this fella's hands.'

The harshness of Hal's tone convinced the raider he had better co-operate.

130

'All right, all right, I'll tell you what you want to know. I could do with a drink myself.'

'Go to hell,' Jennie said when she heard the request. 'The only thing I'll give you is a bullet in the head.' She lifted the pepperbox revolver that had turned the tables on the raiders and looked mean enough to use it.

'All right, Jennie calm down. We need to question this fella. Put that gun away. Start talkin' or I'll take a walk outside and leave you to the mercy of these here girls. I reckon when they've finished with you you'll be beggin' for a bullet in the head.'

17

The coffee was strong and black just the way Hal liked it. He sipped at the large mug, enjoying the aromatic steam from the brew as it tickled his nostrils. With a large Bowie he cut a hunk of bread and deftly topped that with a fried egg. He sliced another hunk and placed that on top of the egg. Already he had managed to munch his way through half the large loaf. He happened to look up and caught Jennie and Kate looking at him with some amusement.

'What . . . ?' he said, the thick sandwich halfway to his mouth.

'Sure would rather keep you a week as a fortnight,' Jennie said admiringly. 'Never saw a fella eat a whole loaf before. What about you, Kate, think he'll finish the loaf?'

The blonde girl was sitting opposite

at the table resting her head on her hand. She and Jennie were sipping coffee. They had not eaten anything. 'I bet you a week's wages he'll finish it,' she said. 'Cowboys ain't used to fresh food. They're like carrion-crows. Mostly they eat coyote and things they find dead on the trail.'

Hal considered her remark for a moment as he bit into the bread. He chewed thoughtfully. 'Mmm . . . I've tasted better. I'm only eatin' this out of politeness. Ma would never have served up this at the table. She would have said this bread is fitten only for the hogs. An' she would have baked another batch.'

The girl's hand came down on the table with a slam. 'Why, you ungrateful slime-toad, I'm famous round these parts for my sourdough. Next time I bake for you I'll use rat-poison.'

'Now, now, you young'uns, settle down. That's no way to start off a relationship,' admonished Jennie.

Kate looked at her with some

indignation. 'Relationship! I'd as soon pal up with a gorilla.'

Hal didn't know how to respond to this jibe. He dropped his gaze and stared at the sheets of paper spread out on the table.

They were the list of names the raiders had brought with them — the so-called death list.

'You recognize any of the names on this paper?' he asked Jennie, trying to steer the conversation away from the hazardous direction it was taking. Somehow he always seemed to end up on the wrong side of the beautiful blonde girl.

Jennie picked the sheet up and studied the names for a moment. 'Oh dear God, these people live all around Peterstown. And my name's here also.' She laid the papers on the table and looked at Hal with widened eyes. 'Does that mean they gonna do what they tried to do here, to all those names?'

Hal glanced over at their captive slumped against the stairway. His hands and feet were fastened together, with the slack looped around a stair-post. Hal had done the roping and then dragged the dead bodies outside and left them in the barn.

'Accordin' to our friend trussed up over there his bunch are only the first of a recruitment drive to bring in gangs of gunmen who'll do just that.' He turned back to the women sitting with him. 'When he was on his deathbed, my pa warned me not to get caught up in this thing. He said war was comin' to Lundon Country. I sorta didn't take much heed of his words at the time. But like or not, I am drawn in. I sure wish I wasn't but I am.'

He heard the horses then, coming up the track. Forgetting his breakfast he grabbed up the shotgun and went across to the front door. 'Douse the light,' he called.

There were soft footsteps behind him and Kate was beside him, her old pistol gripped in her hand.

'You stay back with Jennie,' he

ordered as the light was put out. He opened the door and stared out into the dawn.

Three horsemen spurred into the yard. They hauled up and sat there watching the house. Hal could see all three were holding rifles. In the dim light of the coming dawn he could make out little else.

'Hallo the house,' a voice called.

Hal crouched down inside the doorway, his shotgun aimed at the group of horsemen. To his annoyance Kate had ignored his order to stay inside. She knelt beside him peering out into the yard and holding her pistol in front of her.

'I thought I told you to stay inside,' he hissed, not taking his eyes off the men.

Jennie was at the broken window that Hal had shot out the previous night. 'Who's out there? We're closed for now. Come back tomorrow.'

'Ben Gregory with his two boys. Simon reckons he heard shootin' a while back. He came for me. Is everythin' all right?'

'Ben Gregory, you sure are welcome. Light down and come on in. We had ourselves a mite of trouble sure enough. You better come in an' hear about it.'

Gregory proved to be a tough-looking man with a firm, weather-beaten face. There was several days' stubble on his cheeks. He eyed Hal suspiciously but nevertheless nodded a greeting to him. His sons, Simon, a young man in his late teens, and Tom, not much older, were tall gangly youths obviously overawed by being in this place of ill-repute. They stood awkwardly, not knowing where to look but not wanting to miss anything, casting shy looks at the girls sitting at a table watching the proceedings.

Gregory took in the bloodstains, the bullet-marks and the prisoner tied to the stairs. 'I'll say you had a mite trouble, Jennie.'

'You better come on over here, Ben and see this.'

Jennie led the man to the table. She showed him the paper with the names. Quickly she filled him in with the night's happenings.

'This here is Hal Grant. If it hadn't been for him we might all be hanging from a beam in that barn out there. Hal, this is our nearest neighbour, Ben Gregory and his sons Simon and Tom.'

Gregory was frowning at the paper. 'You serious, Jennie? Surely they ain't mad enough to start a thing like this?'

'They're mad enough,' Hal intervened. 'My pa opposed the plan. He was murdered in Lourdes. Before he died he told me what was afoot. The institute aims to clear out this area of nesters an' farmers. They're convinced the folk of this area are all rustlers an' trouble-makers. Jennie was first on the list but I figure they wanted me as well. One of the men as murdered my father led them here.'

'Here, what am I thinkin' of! Ben, what'll you fellas have to drink?'

'That there coffee sure smells good to me.'

'What about you boys?' Jennie asked the Gregory brothers.

'I'll have a beer, Miss Jennie.'

'Coffee's good enough for them,' Gregory intervened, giving his sons a stern look.

Sheepishly they shuffled forward.

'Sit,' their father ordered and like obedient dogs the boys sat down, though not without casting longing looks towards the girls. The girls for their part were giggling and making suggestive gestures at the boys. Completely out of their depth the boys sat and stared red-faced at the top of the wooden table.

'Coffee.' Kate plonked down the mugs and a fresh pot of coffee.

The Gregory boys grinned up at her, obviously more at ease with the golden-haired caterer. 'Hi, Kate, you workin' late? You need someone to escort you home?'

For reasons he could not understand

a twinge of jealousy was set off in Hal.

'Mmm . . . I'll think about it,' she said impishly, casting a sideways look at Hal and catching his look of displeasure. 'It's so refreshing to meet real gentlemen for a change.'

18

Hal and Kate rode for the most part in silence. Hal was frantically searching for some common topic he could launch into but mostly his mind was taken up with the impending meeting with James Hendron's family. He was afraid to start off on a subject the girl might be able to turn around and use to tease him. He was still at a loss to explain her offer to ride part of the way with him.

'It's on my way home. I can point you in the right direction.'

'You don't live here at the road-house?' he had asked perplexed.

For a few moments she had regarded him with amusement. 'Just because I work here doesn't mean I have to live here,' she replied enigmatically.

The mount she rode had belonged to the raiders killed at the bawdy-house. They had turned the remaining horses in with Jennie's small herd.

Jennie had seen them on their way. 'You call again, Hal Grant. No need to bring any money. Everything's free for you, you hear?'

He had tried in vain to persuade her to uproot and move to somewhere safe.

'This is my home. I been here nigh on twenty years. I don't intend to be scared off by a bunch of cattle-ranchers and their hired killers.'

Ben Gregory had proved a man of action. On being convinced of Hal's legitimate concerns regarding the institute's intentions he had quickly made up his mind on a course of action. 'I reckon I'll get my boys to ride round the neighbours an' warn the folks what's in store for them. I'll stay here to help protect these here ladies in case they try again.'

His boys had protested at the arrangements. 'Pa, why can't we stay an' protect the saloon?'

Gregory had stared his sons straight in the eye and declared it was his boys would need protecting from the girls. Muttering and grumbling they had been sent on their way. He then suggested removing their captive's boots and starting him off in the direction of Peterstown. Seeing the tavern was in good hands Hal and Kate had set out.

They had been riding for some time before the girl reined up her pony. 'That's my place over there.' She pointed to a stand of trees.

A spiral of smoke drifted up from somewhere behind the trees. Hal stared across at where she was pointing.

'You know these Hendrons, then?' he asked at last.

'Sure, I grew up with James — he has a younger brother, Mathew. Their pa was killed in some sort of freak accident a few winters back. They've had a hard time of it since.'

Hal turned and looked up the trail. He felt bad about the news he had to impart to James Hendron's family. More than anything he wanted to turn his horse around and head back to the

Big G, but he had made a promise to a dead man and he couldn't shirk his duty. 'Miss Kate, I need your opinion about somethin',' he said at last.

She waited, sensing his sombre mood. He told her everything about the pursuit of the rustlers and his fatal encounter with James Hendron.

'I know you got a low opinion of me, after all that killin' at the roadhouse an' now I told you it was me as killed James Hendron. I ain't no gunman, Miss Kate, no matter how it looks. Those men followed me to Jennie Fletcher's place to kill me. I had no option but to protect myself.'

She stared squarely back at him with serious eyes. 'I'm inclined to give you the benefit of the doubt,' she said in a low voice. 'When I seen that raider pick up the gun to shoot you I just kept pullin' the trigger of my own weapon. Some of my shots must have hit him. So I'm no different from you, in that respect.'

'Miss Kate, that's mighty big of you

to say that. You acted mighty brave back then.'

She smiled wanly at him without replying to his clumsy attempt to compliment her.

'So you see the pickle I'm in,' he continued. 'I don' know how I'm gonna face Mrs Hendron.'

'You could ride away. You don't need to ever tell her anything.'

Hal looked suitably shocked. 'I made a promise. I can't ride away from that.'

She looked shrewdly up at him. 'I thought you'd say that. Would you like me to come with you?'

He stared hopefully at her, seeing those honest blue eyes gazing out at him. She wore an old battered hat with no band and a brim that drooped over her ears. He thought it gave her the air of a doleful rabbit but refrained from putting his opinion into words.

'Come on home with me. I got to see if auntie is all right. Then you and I'll take a ride over to the Hendrons.'

Auntie proved to be a tough old lady

of indeterminate age. She wore a man's bib and brace and her iron-grey hair was hidden under a hat as decrepit as was her niece's headgear.

''Bout time you brought home a decent fella, Kate Prentice. You look a fine, set-up young man. Are you married or sparkin' a gal?'

'Aunt Gertie,' her niece protested, her face reddening with embarrassment. 'This fella's in trouble, I offered to ride over to the Hendrons and help him out.'

'No matter, don't you let him out of your sight. Good men are hard to come by.'

To try and distract her outspoken aunt Kate told her about the attack on the roadhouse and how Hal had saved the women from being massacred.

'Keep a sharp look-out,' she instructed the old woman. 'If riders come by make sure you know who they are before you show yourself, and keep the gun handy.'

'Sure as hell hope they come round here an' try to mess with Gertie

Althorpe. No man ever got the better of me yet.'

As they rode away the indomitable old lady called after Hal! 'Kate's a fine girl. Just you get your rope on her before some young farmer snatches her up.'

Kate urged her mount to a faster gait in order to get out of range of her aunt's not very subtle matchmaking.

It took her a while to recover her composure, but when she did she began to instruct Hal in the tale he had to relate to Mrs Hendron.

19

'So you see, Mrs Hendron, James saved my life. In doin' so he gave his own.'

Hal was staring at the dirt floor of the sodbuster's dwelling, hating himself for what he had to convey to this worn-out woman.

He had told of an ambush by the men who had killed his father and wanted him dead also. They had wounded him in the side and had him pinned down in a rocky defile and would certainly have shot him to death, only James Hendron had ridden up blazing away with his handgun. Between them they had chased the gunmen away but not before James had taken a fatal bullet.

When he did eventually look up her face was wet with tears.

'If it's any consolation to you the men who shot James have met their just deserts. Those same men followed me to Jennie Fletcher's place. In the ensuin' fight I shot those men to death.'

She rose and walked to an old tin trunk and retrieved from it a well-thumbed book.

'I want to thank you, Mr Grant, for coming here. I know it must grieve you bad to bring such sad news to me.' She opened the book and leafed to the last few pages. 'I want to read you something. It might give you comfort. It surely gives me a certain amount of comfort. I can never read these words without it bringing a tear to my eye.' Looking at the page she began to read. 'It is a far, far better thing that I do, than I have ever done; it is a far, far better rest that I go to than I have ever known.' She looked up at him and he could see a little light of pride shining through the tears. 'Those are the closing words of *A Tale of Two Cities* by Charles Dickens.' She sighed deeply and closed the book. 'Will you stay to lunch with me, Mr Grant?'

'I sure would, ma'am,' Hal rejoined

and could not help adding: 'I had a real poor breakfast.' He deliberately did not look at the girl as he said this.

After a meal of buttered biscuits, molasses and coffee Hal and Kate said their farewells to the grieving woman.

'I always knew James was a good boy,' Mrs Hendron said as she took Hal's hand in hers. 'He was a bit wild. When he did not come home I assumed he had left home for good. Where does he lie now?'

'Mrs Hendron, ma'am, I am sorry to have to tell you I had to leave him where he lay. I said prayers over him as best I could but I was sorely wounded an' had to seek help or I might have died of my wounds. That is why I took so long to seek you out for it was a week or two before I was fit enough to travel. If you like I can take the remains to my ranch and have him buried in the family plot. It's the least I can do. I can have someone come with a buggy and bring you to the Big G when all is ready.'

Hal rode away feeling like a low-down snake. When he looked at Kate riding beside him she could see the misery in his eyes.

'Mr Grant, don't blame yourself for what happened to James. The way you told me it was an accident. You more than made up to him for the way you set his mother's heart at rest.'

'Yeah, by telling her a passel of lies.'

She realized he was not to be consoled. They rode in silence for the rest of the journey.

At the fork in the trail that would take her to her home they stopped and the awkward silence that had accompanied them on the journey seemed set to continue.

'You ride well,' Hal said at last. He pretended to study the horse she was riding. Suddenly he frowned and peered closer at the mount. 'That's the Lazy M brand on that mount,' he exclaimed. For a moment he sat there thinking about his discovery.

'Mr Grant,' she said at last, 'does the

brand mean anything to you?'

'Can you call me Hal? It seems a bit strange for you to call me mister after all we've been through.'

'All right, Hal, but only if you agree to call me Kate.'

'OK Kate, if you insist. The brand on that horse tells me it belongs to a fella called Murphy. It was him as put forward that death list. Pa opposed him and the next thing he was shot down.'

Hal's eyes had turned cold and dark and the girl saw the side of him that contradicted the soft young man who felt so miserable about telling a mother lies in order to protect her from the unsavoury truth about her rustler son.

'Kate, we must part here. If I'm by this way again I would like to call an' say, howdy.' He smiled weakly. 'That is if Auntie Gertie approves of cowboys callin'.'

She looked suitably embarrassed at his reminder of her aunt's forthright remarks. However his words had taken on a more sober tone when he spoke again.

'Kate, you take care. It seems to me those fellas sent out by the ranchers' institute are not too bothered who gets hurt.'

She nodded as she listened to his advice but did not answer.

'So long,' he said and urged his mount forward.

'You take care, Hal,' she said to his back. She sat her borrowed mount and watched him for a long time.

At one point he turned and gazed back at her forlorn figure on top of the big horse. He raised his arm in farewell but she did not respond.

It took him the remainder of the day to reach the Big G and when he alighted, tired and disheartened, he allowed his brother and mother to make a fuss of him. John pestered him with questions but Hal was reluctant to relate the full details of his adventures in front of his mother. It was only later when he and his brother sat on the porch and his mother had retired that he was able to tell John all that had happened.

'Jeez, Hal, this thing is gettin' out of hand. When you first came in I noticed you favourin' your arm but didn't mention it in case it worried Ma.' John was silent for a moment. 'How the hell did they know where to find you? Do you think they're watchin' the house?'

Hal glanced shrewdly at his brother. 'Damn it, John, that thought never occurred to me, so much was happenin'. I just put it down to coincidence.' He stared out into the darkness. 'Spooky to think someone is spyin' on us.' He sighed deeply. 'Anyway, in the mornin' I want to send Francisco out with a wagon to collect the body of poor James Hendron. He knows the location of the rustlers' camp. I can give him rough directions as to where the body might be. If someone goes with him in another buggy an' they find the remains then he can take the buggy on to Grand Hill and bring Mrs Hendron over for the burial.' He rubbed his face tiredly with one hand.

'The body'll be in a bad state after all this time,' John said.

'I know, John, if it's even there any more. But I did promise his mother I would do the right thing an' bring him in for burial.' Hal stood up. 'John, everythin' is such a mess. Nothin's gone right ever since the day I decided to chase up those missin' steers. I got a bad, bad feelin' in my gut. For a bent horseshoe I'd get on my horse and ride away from all this.'

'Hal, don't talk like that. At least you're alive. Poor Pa is dead an' Ma is grievin' sore over him. If anythin' happened to you it'd finish her for sure.'

'I met a gal out there, John, hair yella as corn an' eyes blue as a summer sky.'

'Well, see what I mean. Good things happen as well as bad.'

'She sure puzzles me. She was workin' in a cathouse yet when I made a certain suggestion she slapped me so hard it loosened my teeth.'

John burst out laughing. He laughed so hard that Hal ended up laughing with him. Somehow when he went to bed that night his spirits did not feel so leaden. It was a good feeling to be back among his family again.

20

In the morning Hal made sure Francisco understood what needed doing.

'Take a tarpaulin with you, Francisco. If the body is still there it'll be in a helluva state what with vultures an' coyotes. I'm sorry to ask you to do this but I promised his mother.'

'*Sí*, Señor Hal, the dead do not rest in good health without a proper burial. Do not worry, Señor Hal, I will find heem and bring heem back here.'

Hal watched the wagon pull out, not daring to ask what the Mexican meant by the dead not resting in good health. On John's insistence he saddled up his own mount and rode into Lourdes to visit Doc Patterson to have the wound in his arm seen to. After all that had happened to him in the past few days he wore his Colt and pushed a

Winchester into the saddle bucket.

He was fortunate to find the doctor at home. He, after a careful examination, pronounced his satisfaction with the state of Hal's arm.

'The bullet passed right through the fleshy part of your arm. Whoever cleaned and dressed the wound made a damn good job of it. There's no dirt or sign of any infection. It's healing up nicely.'

The image of Kate was immediately conjured up and Hal felt a warm glow to think that young girl was responsible for the healthy state of the bullet wound.

As a matter of course Doc Patterson also examined the original injury Hal had received in the tussle with the young rustler, James Hendron. He pronounced himself satisfied with the state of both injuries.

'You seem to be in the habit of collecting bullet holes, young man. I don't want to have to treat you for any more. Your pa, God rest his soul, was a good man. It greatly saddened me to see him cut down by a bushwhacker's bullets. I don't want to see his son go the same way.'

Hal was pulling his shirt on and nodded his agreement. 'You're right, Doc. Before he died, Pa warned me to be careful. I'll sure try to keep out of trouble.'

'Have they any leads on the murderous scum that did it to Harry?'

Hal thought a moment before replying. Then he looked the doctor squarely in the eye. 'The men as murdered my father are dead,' he stated sombrely.

The doctor, a sprightly man in his late fifties with a shock of white hair and a ruddy complexion from too much bourbon, looked shrewdly at Hal. 'Folks put you down as a light-headed young wastrel. Looks to me as you're a chip off the old block. Harry Grant was a fine man. He was a strong man and a rich rancher but he never used his power to hurt anyone weaker than himself.' He helped Hal on with his jacket. 'Just you take care, young fella. I don't want to be plugging up any more bullet holes in you.'

He followed Hal into the hallway and watched him strap his pistols in place. 'You ought to take a wife, you know. A good woman can settle a man down. Gives him responsibility and lets him put down roots.'

Hal grinned at the sawbones and before he knew what he was saying he blurted out; 'It was a young woman as bandaged up that wound in my arm.' And then he stopped and coloured up.

'Snap her up, young fella. A girl as can treat a wound like that is a rare find. You clap a bridle on her soonest is my advice.'

Doctor Patterson watched a suddenly embarrassed young man stumble down the steps of his house and wave an awkward goodbye.

'Goddamn it, why did I just say that to Doc?' Hal berated himself as he walked back into town from the doctor's house. All sorts of thoughts were trooping through his mind as he walked. Images of Kate were mixed up with James Hendron and the men he had been forced to kill at Jennie Fletcher's roadhouse. When eventually he stopped he was standing at the spot where his father had been gunned down. He was just opposite Murphy's Emporium.

His father had stepped out for a breath of fresh air when the gunshots had blazed out of the darkness. Though mortally wounded, he had managed to draw his gun and chase off his assailants. They had fled into the darkness to re-emerge at Jennie Fletcher's place in order to assassinate Harry Grant's son. Hal wanted to know who had sent them — who had given the order for the Grants to be eliminated. Hal had an idea he would find some of the answers here at Murphy's.

In spite of his promise to his brother to visit the doctor and then come straight home again, some perverse impulse pushed Hal to cross the road to enter the very place he should have avoided.

Hal walked through the reception area and into the bar. It was barely turned noon yet there were plenty of customers in the place. The bar was lined with drinkers and the tables were fairly full also as people partook of the food that was served at all times of the day and night. Even the bar-girls were active, leaning into the drinkers with low-cut bodices and heavily made-up faces. It reminded Hal of Jennie Fletcher and he momentarily wondered how she and her girls were coping after their ordeal.

No one took any notice of the young cowboy as he found a space at the bar and ordered a beer. He hooked a heel on the brass rail that ran along the bottom of the bar, rested his elbow on the counter behind him and idly watched the crowd.

Hal had never met Stump Murphy but had seen him once or twice when he visited the emporium on some business or other. It had never occurred to him to attend the institute's meetings, leaving that to his father, Harry Grant. Briefly he wondered if he would ever attend now that he knew the direction in which the institute was heading. The idea of wholesale murder was distasteful to Hal and bringing in mercenaries to carry out the dirty work was even more unsavoury. Hal wanted nothing to do with the dealing out of summary justice, moreover his father had warned him away from becoming involved in the dirty business the institute was now mixed up in.

Men were coming and going. From Murphy's point of view the emporium was a thriving concern with the bar and bar-girls and food and gaming-tables bringing in a considerable amount of revenue. There were also the hardware and food-hall and undertaking concerns doing brisk business. Farmers and cowboys were coming and going at all times of the day and night on some errand or other. Very few of them would

163

come in, make a purchase and then leave without stopping for a drink or even a meal. The food was cheap and simple and served piping-hot from the kitchens by a couple of men wearing barkeep aprons, for these waiters also doubled as barkeeps when necessary.

Hal was thinking that Stump Murphy had a lucrative business going here. On top of all this income he also had a sizeable ranch in the Lazy M. Which made him wonder where the horse that Kate had ridden had come from and whether Murphy was directly involved in the murder of his father and the attempted assassination of himself.

Just then a man staggered into the bar. He was dusty and hatless and he wore no boots. Hal recognized the man. He was the surviving raider from the shoot-out at Jennie Fletcher's. He was the man Hal had buffaloed with the stolen shotgun and then roped to the stairs at Jennie's place. He searched his memory for a name and then it came. The leader of the raiders had addressed the man as Barney.

Ben Gregory had kicked Barney out of the roadhouse without boots, weapons or horse. Now he had surfaced at Murphy's Emporium.

21

The man Hal now identified as Barney looked around the barroom, then made for a group of men towards the rear. They were gathered at a table on which were plates of food and beer. They questioned the newcomer for some minutes. One of the diners offered the man a mug of beer, which he drained in one long draught. Licking his lips the man handed back the empty mug and was directed towards the rear of the building. Barney disappeared under an archway with paintings of coffins each side and a logo emblazoned over the top. The words read: Gateway to Heaven.

Hal drifted towards the rear of the saloon. There was so much activity in the place with drinkers and diners and men at the gaming-tables that no one took any notice of him. He loitered by the archway with the painted coffins and then slipped through.

A carpeted hallway led towards the rear. Hal could hear voices. He walked soundlessly down the hall — the carpet deadening his footsteps. A door was ajar and Hal thought it was from behind there that the voices were coming. He stopped and cautiously edged the door wide enough for him to get his head round it and get a view of the interior.

It was a workshop where the coffins were made. Hal could smell wood-shavings and leather and glue all mixed together. A sickly smell of incense overlay everything like a shroud. Coffins were stacked around the room, while others rested on trestles and some propped upright against the walls.

Unlike the rest of the building the room was single-storey and must have been added on at a later date to accommodate the manufacture of coffins. Large skylights in the roof made the room bright enough for the carpenters that laboured here. The voices were coming from the rear of the room. Hal took a chance and slipped inside.

He crouched low behind a couple of unfinished coffins. Now he could make out the voices. Someone was swearing in a harsh tone. Without seeing the men clearly Hal could only guess at their identity.

'Turner an' Partridge returned last night with the same tale as you. That someone shot the hell out of our raidin' party. They reckoned it was a gang lyin' in wait for them, but you say there was but one of them.'

'It was one lone cowboy, probably the one Scoote was after,' another voice replied. 'He bust my head with a shot-gun, then, while I was laid out, he must have killed Lane and Scoote. Turner an' Partridge were upstairs with Jenkins. Jenkins musta come down to see what the fuss was about for he was lyin' on the stairs with his guts blew out the back of his spine. The cowboy hogties me. Then this farmer an' his

168

men ride up 'cos they heard the shootin'. At first they was gonna hang me but instead they took my boots and made me walk into Peterstown. I managed to persuade a fella to give me a lift over here.'

'Goddamn, cowboy, you say. It must be this Hal Grant. What the hell was Lane thinkin' of to let him get the drop on him! Was he foolin' around with the doves? Jesus Christ, he was paid to burn down the whorehouse, not sample its whores.'

The door behind Hal was pushed open and a man stepped inside.

'What the . . . what the hell you doin' there, fella?'

Hal ran a hand along the bottom of the coffin he was crouching behind. 'I was just inspectin' the quality of this here coffin. Was thinkin' of buyin' myself one for my dog. He's gettin' old and I want him to have a decent burial.'

Hal stood and tipped his hat to the man and made to edge past him.

'Not so fast, fella.'

Hearing the exchange the men in the room were coming to see what the fuss was about.

'That's him — that goddamn cowboy I was tellin' you about!'

With quick thinking the man who had discovered Hal slammed the door behind him, blocking his exit. Hal stood back trying to look relaxed. He did not think any action would be taken against him with the busy saloon only yards away.

'Don't know what all the fuss is about. I'm only checkin' over the workmanship. Don't want my dog victim of shoddy design.'

Suddenly a shadow loomed over Hal. He looked up and saw the biggest man he had ever stood up to. Hal was a little over six feet tall. The owner of Murphy's Emporium was equal to Hal in height but his massive breadth of shoulder made Hal look like a slim youth beside him. Three men flanked him, including the one Hal had encountered at Jennie Fletcher's roadhouse. Suddenly

Hal was not so complacent. The five men now facing him all looked decidedly hostile.

'So you're Harry Grant's son,' the big Irishman said, eyeing the young man from beneath lowered eyebrows. 'Seems like you been goin' round shootin' up some men hired by the institute.'

'You mean the murderin' bastards that gunned down my pa and then tried to murder me?' Hal asked, staring coldly back. 'They got their just deserts. I guess I saved a court the bother of tryin' them for murder.'

'Get his guns!'

As he spoke the giant stepped in close and Hal, caught out by the sudden movement, was unable to manoeuvre out of the way. With men surrounding him he stood no chance as they grabbed him and stripped him of his Colts.

'Hold him!'

Hal's arms were grasped and the Irishman swung a punch into his stomach. It was like being hit with a tree-trunk.

Hal gasped and doubled over. He knew he had to move fast if he was to avoid a beating. Bent over as he was with his arms still held by the two henchmen he powered forward and his head cannoned into the Irishman's midriff.

The little group staggered forward as the men holding Hal tried to restrain him. He drove his heel into a booted ankle. Someone swore and then the Irishman recovered enough to swing a punch to Hal's head. Hal was driven backwards. Such was the force of the punch that he saw stars. But as he went back the men pinioning his arms were unbalanced and the whole group fell in an untidy heap.

Hal saw an exposed throat and drove his fist hard and fast into it. The man he hit was gagging and then a boot hit Hal in the side of the head. He was thrown sideways. Frantically he rolled beneath a pair of trestles that held an unfinished coffin.

For a moment he was safe as his

assailants searched for him on the floor. With spinning head he tried to figure out his next move. From his position beneath the coffin he saw the boots coming towards him. With a huge effort he rose to his feet and grasping the bottom of the coffin heaved it mightily towards the oncoming men. They went down with the coffin trapping them beneath it. Hal was on his feet now. The big Irishman was coming towards him with a killing glint in his eyes.

'Damn you!' he roared as he rushed towards the cowboy.

Hal grabbed up the heavy trestle and holding it before him ran towards the big man. They met headlong and the bar of the trestle smashed into the Irishman's teeth as he was coming forward. It did not stop him but blood poured from his mouth and he shook his head and spat out a broken tooth.

'You're dead, Grant.'

Blood was dripping on to the Irishman's shirt as he bellowed out his threat. He grappled with the trestle that was keeping him from his victim. As he tugged Hal suddenly pushed forward and the Irishman was forced to back up as he frantically tried to keep his balance. Unfortunately for him he trampled on one of his men crawling out from under the coffin Hal had hurled moments before, and he went down. Then someone crashed into Hal from the side and he had to give ground under a flurry of punches.

'Get him, you goddamn pansies,' Murphy roared as he dragged himself to his feet. His words were slurred as he tried to get his damaged lips working. He wiped a sleeve across his bloody mouth, then charged forward again with his men flanking him.

Hal was frantically fending off his assailant, then everyone rushed him and he was battling on all fronts. It was an unequal battle and the young cowboy went down under a rain of boots and fists.

'Get him over here.'

Hal was dragged across to a clear

space in the workshop. Two men held him upright as Murphy faced him. Hal watched with some satisfaction as the big man wiped a fist across his face and then peered at the blood on the palm of his hand. The Irishman was breathing heavily and he paused a moment while he regarded the young cowboy. He spat out some more blood.

'I'll tell you what's gonna happen to you, cowboy. I'm gonna beat you to a pulp. You won't be quite dead, just barely conscious. Then we're gonna give you a proper funeral just as if you were really dead. You'll be nailed up in one of these here coffins. You can even have your pick if you are in any fit state to make a choice. Then we'll load you into the hearse and take you out to Boot Hill.' The big man swayed unsteadily and wiped at his mouth again. 'We'll bury you nice and deep so's nobody can hear you screamin'. And while you suffocate you can ponder on the foolishness that brought you to try an' stand against Stump Murphy.'

22

Hal blinked blood out of his eyes. 'I can tell you're a real man, Murphy. Were you run out of Ireland for chicken-stealin'? You can't face me man to man but need these hirelin's to help you. Yes, I killed those men you sent after me. An' I'll kill you too if you tell these hound-dogs of yours to back off while I pound you to a jelly.'

'Hah!' The Irishman looked with some surprise at Hal.

The young man's face was bleeding and his arm was soaked in blood where the recently bandaged wound had been opened again. He looked hardly fit to walk never mind carry out his threat to kill the man in front of him. With sudden fury he backhanded Hal across the face. Hal's head jolted sideways with the force of the blow. Then stung by Hal's taunts to kill him Murphy paused.

'Let him go,' he said, 'I'm gonna enjoy poundin' this young upstart into an early grave.'

Hal almost managed to avoid the wild swing that would have carried his head off his shoulders if it had landed properly. The huge fist grazed the side of his face and he felt as if a piece of granite had abraded the skin of his cheek. He drove a punch at the big target in front of him that the Irishman seemed not to notice. A boot came from behind and hit him on the small of the back and he soon realized that in spite of the Irishman's protestations this was not going to be a fair fight. He was still fighting five men inside the carpentry shop.

The kick drove him on to the big meaty fist and again he saw stars as his ear took the full impact. He staggered sideways and was prevented from going down by a brawny pair of arms that wrapped round from behind him. Hal saw the fist coming at him again and with the strength of a desperate man he swung out of the way. He heard a gasp as the man holding him took the blow meant for him. The arms clamped round him were suddenly released.

Hal did not see what happened to the man, for he was desperately trying to avoid another wild punch. He blundered in among a batch of coffins. The remainder of the men were crowding round, prevented from inflicting more damage on their victim by the confines of the surroundings. A boot hit Hal on the thigh. And a punch crashed into his face. In spite of his determination Hal went down. Desperately he rolled away from the barrage of boots that seemed to be coming from all directions.

'Leave him, he's mine!' Hal heard Murphy roar at his henchmen.

As he scrabbled on the floor he saw a wooden handle covered in dust. It had obviously fallen to the floor and been undetected for some time. Hal grabbed the wood thinking to use it as a stabbing tool. It was more than a wooden handle. The thing was a wood chisel sharpened to a razor-edge by a craftsman who knew how to keep tools in good condition.

The big fist was swinging at the helpless victim. Behind it was Murphy's grimace as he sought to finish the young cowboy. Hal drove the steel blade at the big knob of bone and gristle that was aiming to knock him unconscious. The blade cut into flesh and penetrated into the bony knuckles. The Irishman jerked back astonished by the sudden pain. His mouth opened and he roared in agony. Hal did not waste time wondering at the damage he had done. Using the chisel as a stabbing-tool he drove it with all his strength into the leather boot just in front of him. Such was the force of Hal's thrust the blade went through leather and down into bone and almost out the other side. So far in did the blade penetrate the tool was wrenched from Hal's grip as the Irishman fell back roaring in pain.

Momentarily, the felling of their champion stunned his men. Hal was not so complacent with his sudden victory. Already he was looking round for another weapon. He did not see one but he did see an avenue of escape from this tight spot.

A window with blackened panes caught his attention. A freestanding coffin-lid smashed into the frame and glass showered out into the daylight. Hal dived through the window after the coffin-lid. He landed awkwardly and lay winded for a moment before the drive for survival had him on his feet and running for the safety of the front street. As he hit the street he was momentarily bewildered by the comparative normality of the scene.

Horses stood placidly tied up outside the emporium. Wagons and buggies were parked in the wagon-park. Vehicles drove peacefully by on the street as the bloody, dishevelled figure staggered along the boardwalk towards the livery. Hal found it hard to imagine that just a few yards away he had fought for his life against Murphy and his thugs.

Because he had intended only to walk to the doctor and get patched up, which he figured would take only a very short time, Hal had left his mount fully saddled at the livery. Painfully he pulled himself into the saddle. With rage and just anger surging inside he wrenched the reins and headed back down towards the emporium. As he rode he removed his Winchester from the saddle bucket. Outside Murphy's Emporium he turned the horse's head and aimed it at the big double doors.

The sudden commotion at the entrance brought everyone's head around. They stared in amazement at the young cowboy with blood streaming down his face and bloody clothes as he clattered into the building atop his pony. In his hands was a Winchester rifle. Almost as one man the customers dived for the floor as the rifle began to fire.

Hal blasted away at mirrors and chandeliers. Bottles exploded as the bullets riddled the bar. A piano gave a few plaintive notes as bullets wreaked havoc inside the workings. From that day it never played without a plaintive quiver, as if afraid that another attack was about to be made on its workings.

With anger still seething within him Hal wrenched his mount's head around and clattered out of the building, leaving behind terrified costumers and hundreds of dollars' worth of damage. He left because his rifle was empty and his only other weapons were lying in the rear of the building, in the possession of the owner of the wrecked emporium.

23

'For God's sake, Hal, what are you — a one-man crusade out to right the wrongs of the world?'

'Ouch,' was Hal's only reply as his mother pressed a little too hard with the damp cotton on a cut above his eyebrow.

His brother John paced the kitchen floor, a worried frown on his face as he berated his battered sibling. Though John was younger than Hal by a couple of years he took it on himself to be his brother's counsellor.

'You realize what you've done? Murphy represents the institute — I mean the Institute of Wyomin' Ranchers. By goin' against him you're settin' yourself against every rancher in the area. First you go out to Peterstown an' gun down God knows how many of their hired hands an' now you go into the lion's den an' shoot up Murphy's place of business.'

Hal's mother rinsed the cotton in the basin of water that had taken on a pinkish tinge as she worked on the cuts and abrasions on his face. Steam rose gently into the air and for a moment all that could be heard was the trickle of water back into the basin as she squeezed the surplus water from the cloth. She went back to work on Hal's face.

'You know we're members of the institute, Hal, now that Pa's gone? Tell me how we can ride in an' attend a get-together at Murphy's place now? The hand of every man on that committee will be against us.'

John stopped his pacing and glared at his brother.

'You finished now?' Hal asked him.

'No, I am not finished . . . ' John began but his brother held up his hand to silence him.

'Just let me say my piece an' then you can rant an' rave as much as you like.

184

But I'm gettin' a damn headache listenin' to all that nonsense you been spoutin'. This war is not of my choice. Pa could see trouble loomin' and warned me to stay clear. I figured to take his advice. Then Murphy sent those killers after me an' I was in the trouble up to my neck.'

'You can't say Murphy sent those gunhands after you,' John interrupted. 'Did any of them admit to anythin'?'

'Jesus Christ, John, grow up. He damn well admitted it to me when he thought he had me corralled back there in Lourdes . . . ouch! Go easy, Ma, that hurt.'

'Then moderate your language, Hal Grant. I may be an old widowed woman but I'm still your mother. Now if you want to talk to your brother, then do it in a civilized manner. The next swearword I hear from you I . . . I'll take a pan and batter some respect into that stubborn head of yours.'

John was caught out grinning at Hal as his mother swung round to him.

'And wipe that smile off your face, you grinning jackass. That goes for you too. You're not too old for me to take your britches down and tan your hide for you.'

It was Hal's turn to grin at his brother's discomfiture but he quickly set his face to normal when his mother turned her attention back to him.

'Your father always stood for fairness and justice,' Allison Grant stated before the brothers could return to their debate. 'I seen it all before. When bad men want something unlawful there is no deed they'll not stoop to. Though I don't believe in the law of the gun there comes a time in a person's life when they must decide whether to let the evildoers carry on with their vile ways or to stand up and oppose them. Hal is right, John. If all he says is true then he had no option but to face down the Murphy gang. They murdered your father and tried to do the same to Hal. If they manage to kill Hal, which God forbid, then you will be their next target unless you decide to forgive and forget and join them in their wicked schemes. And that is something I hope I never live to see from a son of Harry Grant.'

There was a profound silence in the kitchen when their mother ceased speaking. Her lips were drawn in a prim line and she returned to the tending of her son's cuts. 'That's all. You can continue arguing now. I've said my piece.'

'There's nothin' more to say after that, Ma. You've about laid it all out for us. We can't back down from this or we'll be always lookin' over our shoulders wonderin' where the next bushwhacker is lyin' in wait. Pa said the war was comin' an' warned me to stay out of it. I ain't got that choice now.'

The sound of wagon wheels prevented any more discussion. John left the kitchen to find out what the arrival of a vehicle heralded and left Hal and his mother alone. She laid the blood-discoloured cotton down and took her son's face in her hands.

'You're so much like your father, Hal. He would never run away from a fight. Though I fretted and worried about him when he was in danger I was proud to be married to such a strong upright man.' She smiled fondly at him. 'You know your father worried that you were going to grow up a wastrel. He knew different before he died. He grew real proud of you and what a fine man his son was growing up to be.' She leant down and kissed him on the forehead. 'Just you be real careful, son. I don't want to be burying any more of my menfolk out in that plot.'

Hal placed his hands on his mother's waist and smiled up at her. 'Don't you worry about me, Ma. I'll be around the Big G for a long time to come.'

'Get yourself a good woman, Hal. Put down some roots.'

'You know, Ma, Doc Patterson gave me the same advice earlier on today. I guess I must be gettin' old.'

She drew her son's head into her bosom and held him quietly like that.

Footsteps sounded in the hall and John put his head round the door.

'Francisco has returned with that cargo you sent him after. An' he has a wagonload of women in tow as well.'

Hurriedly Hal followed his brother outside.

'Well, as I live an' breathe if it ain't Hal Grant. Howdy, fella, if it don't do a gal's heart good to see you again.'

Hal gaped as Jennie Fletcher and her girls clambered chattering and laughing from out of the buggy. On the next wagon Franciso saluted with his whip. Then another buggy drew alongside. This was the one he had sent out to collect Mrs Hendron if the mission to recover her son's body was successful. In the buggy were two women. Both women were dressed in black — one elderly and careworn, the other younger and looking extremely beautiful, her black cape a perfect contrast to the golden hair spilling out from underneath.

Embarrassed and flustered and not

knowing what to say Hal stepped down from the porch to greet the visitors. He turned and looked helplessly at his mother who was standing behind him also looking faintly bemused.

Within moments a quiet afternoon at the Big G was turned upside down as mourners disembarked for the funeral of James Hendron.

24

Mrs Grant was not a woman to be discomfited for long by a sudden influx of visitors, no matter how odd they might appear.

'Hal, bring the ladies inside to the parlour. I'll get drinks going and then you can make the introductions.' With a generous wave of her arms and a friendly smile Hal's mother included everyone in her hospitality.

John was grinning from ear to ear as he watched his brother floundering in the veritable flood of female company. 'This way ladies, there's room for everyone inside,' he called, hugely enjoying himself.

Chattering excitedly and eyeing up the brothers with fluttering lashes and inviting smiles the doves trooped inside past a bewildered Hal.

'Mrs Hendron, Miss Kate.' Hal was

left to escort the two women from the last buggy.

Smiling brightly Kate glided past Hal and disappeared inside. When Hal accompanied Mrs Hendron into the parlour the blonde girl was nowhere to be seen.

In the kitchen Mrs Grant was rushing round putting kettles on for coffee and looking in despair in her pantry to see what she could rustle up for her guests when an extremely beautiful blonde girl stepped into the kitchen and introduced herself.

'Mrs Grant, I take it you are Hal's mother. I'm Kate Prentice. I met Hal on his visit to Peterstown. I appreciate this is all a great imposition on you. My aunt will be arriving shortly with provisions for to feed the funeral party. She'll also be bringing along the preacher, Reverend Murcott.' Kate undid her cloak and hung it on a hook behind the door. 'In the meantime we can be baking a few biscuits and making coffee.'

In a very short time Mrs Grant found herself playing second fiddle to this competent young girl as she mixed dough and helped dispense drinks to the assembly. As she worked the girl chattered away to the older woman and Mrs Grant found herself warming to this lovely young girl.

'You see, Mrs Grant, Jennie is a very soft-hearted woman. When she heard that young James Hendron was dead and his mother had to travel all the way over here to bury him she rallied round and insisted the girls accompany her so the poor woman would not feel so lonely.'

Mrs Grant smiled. 'I take it those ladies my boys are entertaining in the parlour are working girls.'

'Indeed, Mrs Grant, but don't let that bother you too much. They have hearts of gold. They could have refused to come but they all knew James and they wanted to give him a decent send-off. When they heard that Hal was prepared to organize the funeral for poor Mrs Hendron they wanted to do something to show their appreciation for what Hal had done for them.'

'Hal, my Hal done for them?' Mrs Grant asked with raised eyebrows.

Kate glanced quickly at the older woman. 'He didn't tell you about the raid on the roadhouse?'

'He told me there was some bother when some men tried to kill him. The same men, I might add, who shot his father to death.'

'Oh, Mrs Grant, I am sorry. I heard about it from Hal but it was thoughtless to bring it to mind again. It must still be very painful for you.'

'Tell me about the roadhouse.'

So Kate told her how Hal, almost single-handedly, had foiled the raiders and saved Jennie Fletcher and her girls from certain death. 'He was so strong and brave,' Kate said wistfully, not realizing the whole story of her feelings was showing in her face.

'Hal, so like his father,' Mrs Grant said then, after a pause, 'I suppose you work at the roadhouse too?'

Kate saw the pitying look the woman gave her. She walked across to the older woman and took her hands in hers. 'I do work there, Mrs Grant, but not in the way you think. I live with my Aunt Gertie. She took me in when my parents died. She hasn't much, only a good heart, and she struggled to bring me up decent. I work at the roadhouse as a cook to make ends meet. With the money I make there and the food we grow ourselves we keep going. No matter what people think I'm not ashamed of what I do.'

The look of anguish on the older woman's face made Kate smile widely. Then Mrs Grant pulled the girl to her and hugged her hard.

'I'm sorry, so sorry, Miss Prentice, I'm just an ignorant old woman.'

That was how Hal found them when he poked his head inside the kitchen wondering what had happened to the golden-haired girl. He had just learned from Jennie Fletcher that it was Kate's idea to give James Hendron a proper send-off.

'Ahem,' he said, slightly embarrassed to find his mother and Kate in an affectionate embrace. 'Your aunt has arrived, Miss Kate. She says she needs some help with the candies and cakes you baked for the funeral feast.'

Instead of being embarrassed the two women smiled at Hal and then grinned at each other. 'Let's go,' said Hal's mother, looking more cheerful than Hal had seen her since the death of her husband. 'Let's feed these delightful young women.'

The Reverend Murcott was a jolly young man with a shining red face, a paunch and a balding head. By the time the party of doves and cowboys and chief mourners had gathered a grave had been dug in the Grant family burial plot. The ranch handyman had quickly put together a rough-hewn coffin.

'Dearly beloved, we are gathered here today to send a young man off to a life he will find infinitely better than the short, harsh existence he experienced in this world. James Hendron was but young in years but large in heart.' The sky pilot looked round at the assembly, taking in everyone with his ingenuous smile. 'I imagine James is looking down at this funeral right now and thinking, what a popular fella I was. It is my role to thank you on his behalf for coming here today to give solace to his grieving family.'

Hal thought there was something so uplifting about the preacher's words that the guilt he felt at his role in the young rustler's death lightened somewhat.

'Mrs Hendron asked me to recite a quote from Dickens. I believe it is fitting that she read that out herself. I will content myself with a couple of lines from one of William Shakespeare's sonnets. *They look into the beauty of thy mind, And that in guess they measure by thy deeds.*'

The preacher smiled encouragingly at Mrs Hendron and she stepped forward and with quavering voice spoke the words she had read out to Hal when he had last visited her to tell her of the death of her son. Hal could hear some women weeping as she finished.

'Let's send James off with a rousing hymn. I'll start us off but I want to hear everyone singing. Don't worry if you don't know the words. Just hum as loud as you can. The hymn I have picked I feel is very appropriate for the dear departed.'

Reverend Murcott started singing in a rich baritone and after some hesitation the voices around the grave joined in.

Blest are the pure in heart,
For they shall see our God . . .

25

Harvey Baker could not help staring in some wonderment at Stump Murphy. The man's face was swollen and discoloured with bruises, his mouth was a mess of scabbed-over cuts. Occasionally when Murphy grimaced or talked Baker noticed teeth missing or broken in the man's mouth. On top of that Murphy sat on a chair with a heavily bandaged food elevated on a stool.

'What the hell you starin' at?' the Irishman snarled.

'Huh.' Baker was startled and dropped his eyes, not knowing how to react.

'Say what you have to say an' then get the hell outta here.'

Hal Grant's ranch hand hurriedly told Murphy about the funeral taking place out at the Big G. Very quickly he had Murphy's attention.

'You say Jennie Fletcher an' her

whores are out there, now?'

'Yeah, they brung a preacher for the burial service. I don't know why they're buryin' the fella in the family graveyard. Some of his folk have travelled over for the funeral.'

'What's this dead fella's name?'

'James Hendron. I overheard that much but other than that I don't know much about him.'

'Hendron.' Murphy took up a sheet of paper and studied it for a moment. Then he let out a grunt. 'James Hendron — Grand Hill Farm, that's one of the names on the list.' He pursed his broken lips for a moment as he tapped his forefinger on the paper.

Only then did Baker realize that the Irishman's hand was also bandaged. He would dearly have loved to know what happened to wreak such injuries on the saloon owner but was prudent enough to know that such an enquiry would be a dangerous one to pursue.

'And they're still out there at the Big

G?' Murphy suddenly snapped at the ranch hand.

'Yeah, I rode over here straight away. I thought you would want to know, especially as it was over at the whorehouse your men bought it. How is Scoote, anyway? The last time I saw him his face was all cut up.'

Baker wished he could have bitten off his tongue before voicing his query after the gunman. The Irishman looked at him suspiciously for a moment, wondering whether some hidden jibe was aimed at his own battered face.

'Scoote's dead along with three or four others who were sent over to Jennie Fletcher's to finish the job. Seems your boss, Grant, jumped them an' the ones he didn't kill he sent flyin' with their tails between their legs. There must be some tie-up between Grant an' that whore queen. I see a way here to get back at that sumbitch.' The Irishman eyed the man in front of him speculatively. 'He sweet on one of those doves, you think?' he asked.

Baker shrugged. 'Maybe,' he said noncommittally. 'Now you ask, he seemed mighty friendly with one in particular — a flaxen-haired gal. Sure is a beauty.' He screwed up his eyes in thought. 'Name of Kate — didn't catch her last name. She came in with the Hendron fella's mother.'

There was silence as the saloon owner brooded over this information, seeking some edge that would bring Grant into his power. He was still incensed over the damage that had been wrought by one lone cowboy. Suddenly he came to a decision. He took out a wad of notes and counted some off before handing them to Baker.

'Here, that's for your trouble. Now, ride out to the Lazy M and rouse up my foreman, Ronald Preston. Tell him to kit up as many men as he can muster for to ride out to Jennie Fletcher's. He's to put Nathaniel Stone in charge of the riders. Tell him the roadhouse should be empty. I want them to take over the entire premises. They're to lie in wait for anyone comin' back to the place.' The saloon owner watched the cowboy stuff the money into a pocket. 'Then tell Preston to wait out at the ranch for me. I want him for a special job. You got all that?'

'Sure, Mr Murphy, I'll take care of it.'

'Make sure you get it right,' Murphy snarled. 'Any messin' up and you'll finish up like Scoote an' company.' He eyed the ranch hand with some distaste. 'After tonight you'll be needin' another job; there'll more 'n likely be an openin' for you at the Lazy M.'

Baker nodded, trying to look grateful, and waited patiently to be dismissed.

'Well don't hang about there like a constipated hen,' the big man growled. 'Oh, one more thing. On your way out tell Barney to get my rig ready. I'll be followin' you out to the Lazy M. I can see I have to take personal charge of the next phase of tonight's operation. It looks if I want anythin' done I have to do it myself.'

Baker hurried out from the rear office glad to be away from the uncertain temper of the saloon owner.

★   ★   ★

'Hal Grant, I want to thank you for this day of respect you arranged for my dear departed son.'

Mrs Hendron stood looking up at Hal with tear-bright eyes. The farewells were being said. Cowhands who had been hanging around the bunkhouse when the funeral had begun were now chatting to Jennie Fletcher's girls and arranging assignations. Hal and his mother and John were in a little group with Mrs Hendron and Kate and her aunt.

'My heart is not so sore as when I set out this morning.' The grieving mother turned to Mrs Grant. 'You have a fine son there, Mrs Grant.' Then she smiled at John. 'Two fine young men, I should say. Take care of them. I envy you your good family and wish you long life to enjoy them.'

The women embraced and Hal looked at Kate and smiled at her. Then Hal's mother embraced and kissed Kate and her aunt.

'Thank you, Miss Kate, for coming over and helping out,' she said, holding the girl at arm's length and smiling at her.

Kate smiled brightly and nodded, casting a sideways look at Hal as she did so. For him it was a ray of sunshine beaming out of the dark habit she had donned for the sombre occasion.

It was an emotional parting all around.

'I'll ride a part of the way with you,' Hal said impulsively.

'Why, I'd better ride along and look after you, big brother,' John called mischievously. 'What with your reputation with women I can't risk all these females out there alone with you.' For John had seen how Hal and Kate were shyly eyeing each other and felt a little twinge of jealousy, for he quite fancied the lovely golden-haired girl for himself.

Kate for her part looked askance at Hal when she heard John's observation about Hal's reputation with women, then she turned and walked to the buggy that was to carry them home. Hal glared at John who looked innocently back at him.

'What the hell you mean by that remark?' he hissed.

'I thought it was you as invited all these females to the funeral is all I meant. Only a man with charisma and charm could attract so many females. They swarm about you like flies to a cow-chip.'

'Keep your smartass remarks to yourself,' Hal said testily. He stalked off to get his horse.

It was a noisy and jolly little party that left the Big G ranch house. The roadhouse girls were waving and calling to the cowboys who, seeing their boss accompanying the buggies, raced to get mounted so they too could ride part of the way with the funeral party. Hal did not look too pleased but there was nothing he could do as almost the entire male population of the Big G escorted the ladies of leisure on their departure.

Far ahead in the fading day another party was riding hard towards the same destination. There were at least a dozen riders. All were male and wore long duster coats with slouch hats and were well-armed with rifles and pistols and a sprinkling of shotguns. It was a formidable force by any account.

26

Ronald Preston stared after the horsemen as they headed away from the Lazy M. A normally dour man anyway, the foreman of Murphy's Lazy M looked even more sombre as he contemplated the happenings of the last half-hour. Harvey Baker, a Big G ranch hand, had ridden up and told him Murphy had sent instructions for the foreman to kit out Stone and his men. Then he told him of their mission. Preston knew the Big G ranch hand by sight and wondered why and how Murphy had recruited him.

The foreman of the Lazy M ranch did not much like the cruel, hard-faced men that he was forced to house and feed. They kept themselves separate from the ordinary cowboys who worked the ranch for Preston and his boss.

His own instructions had been

straightforward. He was to provide mounts and provisions for the mercenaries camped on his ranch. Stone was to take his well-armed force and ride to Jennie Fletcher's whorehouse and take over the place. He was then to lie in wait for the party of females to return and take them prisoner and anyone else who happened along.

Ronald Preston hawked and spat and stared off into the distance. He approved the plan set up by the Institute to raid the smallholdings which were suspected of cattle-rustling and warn them off. It looked as if things were coming to a head. He just hoped it would all be over soon. It was not his job to question the motives of his boss but the presence of the hired gun-hands on the Lazy M was unsettling to the ordinary ranch hands. He walked across to the corral and roped and saddled a mount while waiting for his boss to arrive.

★   ★   ★

The Grant family were gathered in the dining-room discussing the day's events. John was busy teasing his brother.

'You're a dark horse, Hal, keepin' all those females to yourself. I begin to wonder if you got those bullet holes and beatin's from irate husbands an' boyfriends.'

'John, if you don't lay off me I won't be responsible for what I end up doin' to you.'

John nodded sagely. 'Guilty conscience makin' you tetchy. Mind you, I can't blame you for keepin' that there Kate Prentice hush-hush. She's a real looker. Think I might just ride over to her place an' ask her auntie if I could start walkin' out with her.' John nodded to an imaginary girl on his arm. 'Evenin' Miss Kate, I come to see if I can put my brand on you.' A well-aimed book flying straight for his head spoilt his comic performance.

'John, so help me, I'll swing for you,' Hal fumed, touched by a jealousy that was unsettling.

'Hal, that's enough,' admonished Mrs Grant. 'And John, will you leave your brother alone. You're like a pair of big kids. If I had the strength I'd take down your britches and spank you both.' She got up and retrieved the book. 'You'd be better off reading books instead of throwing them at each other.' She studied the spine of the book. '*Boys of Green Mountain* — that's one of my favourite novels! I'll not have you abusing books, Hal Grant.'

'Sorry, Ma,' Hal said, chastened by his mother's chagrin. 'It's been a worriesome day.'

'Worriesome or not, does not give you an excuse for bad behaviour.' She paused for a moment. 'Though John is right about one thing; your friend, Kate Prentice, is a lovely young girl. I made a terrible mistake with her. I assumed she worked at the . . . the . . . at Jennie Fletcher's place as a . . . well, you know what I mean.' The brothers watched in wonderment as their mother coloured up, embarrassment overwhelming her. 'Anyway she was so charming about it all. She assured me she worked as a cook for Jennie. Said Jennie was very kind and told her half the attraction at the roadhouse was the fine food she set up for the clients. It was an awful thing I said to the girl but she was so nice about it. I told her she was welcome to visit at any time.'

Mrs Grant looked defiantly at her sons as if she expected them to berate her for being so free with her invitations. Before her sons could make a reply there came a knocking on the front door.

'Golly, that'll be Miss Prentice, now,' quipped John with a mischievous twinkle in his eye. 'She's a fast worker.'

Hal threw his brother an irritated look as he rose to answer the knock.

'Boss, there's a fella here wants to speak to you.'

Hal stepped out into the porch and looked at the man and for a moment did not recognize him. 'Howdy, what can I do for you?'

The man stepped forward. Hal's eyes narrowed as he recognized the foreman of the Lazy M standing before him with his hat in his hand. He nodded at Hal.

'Howdy, Mr Grant, I need to talk to you about somethin' important.'

'I'm listenin'.' There was no warmth in Hal's reply. He watched as the man shuffled uncomfortably.

'I shouldn't be here, you know that.'

Hal did not reply but waited for Murphy's foreman to speak. The man shifted uncomfortably and hesitated.

'I don't want to be overheard. I shouldn't be here at all. I'm riskin' my job an' maybe even my life comin' out here.'

In spite of himself Hal was intrigued. 'Wait here,' he said. Then he went back to the house and stepped inside the kitchen.

'John, Ronald Preston's outside wantin' to talk to me.' John's eyes widened but before he could say anything Hal continued: 'He seems a bit edgy. I'm goin' down the yard a piece with him. I want you to shadow us. Try not to be seen. He might be on the up and up or it might be a trick to get me on my own an' count coup on me for his boss.'

When Hal came out of the house again he had his gun stashed in the back holster.

'Let's walk,' he said curtly. The two men ambled down the yard to the corral. Hal leaned his back against the top bar and gazed at his companion. His hands were hooked in his back pockets, ready to make a fast draw if Preston made a false move.

'I heard what you did to Mr Murphy,' Preston said as he stopped alongside Hal. 'An' I seen the results. He's hoppin' mad over it. He wants to get even. That part I can understand. It's . . . it's the next bit of the plan that sticks in my craw.' The man pulled a tobacco plug from his top pocket and offered to share it with Hal. When the youngster declined the foreman bit into the plug and worried it with his teeth till he detached a chunk suitable for chewing. For a moment he worked this while Hal waited patiently.

'Your man ain't very subtle, sneakin' about keeping a watch on me,' he said at last. 'After all that's happened I don't blame you for being suspicious of anyone from my side of the fence.'

Hal sighed. 'Come on up here, John. You're about as clumsy as a buffalo looking out for its calf.'

John came up out of the yard and grunted a greeting, obviously peeved at being caught out.

'I ain't come out here to gun you down, Mr Grant. I came to warn you of somethin' as is happenin' over in Peterstown. I don't stand for rustlin' but I don't stand for killin' females neither.'

Hal tensed. 'What the hell you on about, Preston?'

'That roadhouse where you shot up those hired guns is still the target for the Institute. They believe if they shut down Jennie Fletcher then the main outlet for stolen beeves will be closed. So in the mornin' they're sendin' another crew out there with orders to put the whorehouse outta business once an' for all.'

Hal had come off the fence. 'You said somethin' about killin' females?'

'That's the bit I couldn't stomach. Them there gunnies have orders to kill everyone they find out at the road-house.'

27

The Sheep Dip saloon in Peterstown was packed to the doors and yet men still pushed in. The taciturn barkeep who had misdirected Hal was kept busy serving up drinks. For once his red, sweaty face looked faintly less bad-tempered as he took coin over the bar.

Ben Gregory stood on a chair and called for silence. No one took any notice of him. Again he yelled for order.

'Goddamn might as well talk to a herd of steers as get any sense out of this mob,' he muttered. In desperation he pulled his pistol and fired a shot into the ceiling. Several things happened. Some men tried to get to the door, some threw themselves on to the floor, but most looked towards the source of the shot. A reasonable silence fell on the crowd as they saw Ben atop his chair. A cloud of dust drifted from the ceiling on to the rancher.

'That's better. A fella can hardly hear hisself speak. You're like a clutch of chickens in a hen coup, there's so much cluckin' goin' on.'

Someone started to cheer and a lot of men joined in. Ben Gregory was well-liked and respected and it was an affectionate cheer that went up from the assembled men.

The crowd was made up of the local ranchers and sodbusters from the surrounding area. They had one thing in common: a constant struggle against poverty. Life was an ongoing battle against disease in livestock, crop failure, drought, floods or pests. When Ben Gregory called for a meeting almost all had responded as it meant an evening's relief from the unremitting struggle to keep a roof over their family and food on the table. They had seen good men buckle under the strain of subsistence living and pack up and leave. Each such event was another dent in their determination to persevere.

'Hey, Ben there's stardust in your hat,' someone called as dust continued to settle on to his head.

'That ain't stardust, that's grey matter,' someone else quipped.

'Listen up, you fellas, you'll all be dust in the ground if you don't take heed of what I have to say.' Ben held up a piece of paper. 'You know what this is?'

'It's your last will an' testament,' a voice called.

There was a gale of laughter.

'Leave me your missus, Ben, she's sure a looker and a hard worker.'

'I'll trade you mine for a good milker any day,' another voice called.

Ben was getting red in the face. 'Damn you, will you listen?' He shook the paper in the air. 'This here is a death-list drawn up by the Institute of Wyomin' Ranchers. Shall I read you the names?' Not giving any time for interruptions he held the paper in front of his face and began reading. 'John Wilson, Terence Perkins, Josiah Madison, Patrick Mellen . . . '

The crowd stilled as Ben read on without pause. Name after name was called out. Most of the named men were present. An uneasy silence grew in the room, broken only by Ben's litany of men sentenced to death with the sanction of the Institute of Wyoming Ranchers. Relentlessly Ben recited the names. By the time he had finished, the room was completely quiet. He lowered the paper and looked expectantly at the crowd. There was no joking now. Men glanced uneasily at their neighbours, then looked away, seeing fear and anxiety mirrored in their faces. Then the shouting began.

'That can't be true! No one has the authority to kill us.'

'We are citizens with rights! We ain't broke no laws!'

'What they wanna do that for anyway? What we done to deserve it?'

Ben stood quietly waiting for the shouters to run out of steam, then he raised his hand for silence. 'It's started already. The Institute has hired gun-fighters to carry out their dirty work for them. They raided Jennie Fletcher's place a night or two ago. A bunch of them came in and killed young Jim Sanger, the kid as worked for Jennie. They also gunned down Horse Kearney, Joe Poison and Jack Talbot. Only a cowboy name of Hal Grant was there at the time an' got the drop on them, or the death toll would'a been a lot higher.'

'But why! Why'd they wanna take it out on Jennie an' her girls?'

'You know Jennie. When you go for a drink there how do you pay? There's a lot that pays with a few rustled head of cattle. An' as well as that, they probably thought Jennie's whorehouse was an easy target. An' it would have been if this Grant hadn't happened along. Just think about it. By hangin' Jennie and her girls it sends out a deadly message to the rest of you an' it sure as hell stops one outlet for rustled cattle.'

This caused another outburst. Clenched

fists were waved in the air. Men shouted out — some in anger and some in fear. Ben had a hard time quietening the mob.

'The thing is,' he called when the shouting had subsided, 'what we gonna do about it?'

'What can we do? We're just farmers, we ain't gunfighters. How can we go up against hired gunmen?'

'You're men, ain't you?' replied Ben. 'All of you have a weapon of some kind. Most of you go huntin' from time to time. If you can shoot a deer you sure as hell can shoot a man on a horse when he comes up to your farm to kill you an' your family.'

'The hell with that! What chance has one man against a bunch of gunslicks! I'm for pullin' out. Been thinkin' about it for some time. Now's as good a time as any. Can't make much of a livin' nohow in this Godforsaken country.'

'You can't just quit! You got rights. No man should be driven out of his home.'

'What rights will I have swingin' on the end of a rope as Ben says they aim to do to us?'

'We can send for the marshal. We got the law on our side.'

'Hell! The marshal's two days' ride away in Toska. Two days there an' two days back, if he comes at all. By that time this could be a wasteland.'

'Ain't right! We ought to do somethin' to stop them big ranchers!'

The discussion raged as frightened men contemplated an uncertain future. They were simple men used to hard work and hard times. They weren't used to guns and gunmen and ruthless ranchers — ranchers who had no concept of what it meant to wring a bare living from the land with hardly any resources.

The wealthy ranchers wanted rid of the small farmers who fenced off the land to grow their crops. It was land the rancher coveted for his own use. For it had provided free grazing until the farmers had been given grants to cultivate and settle. The wealthy usually took what they wanted from the weak and if the underdog objected then the resources of the moneyed classes were always sufficient to hire guns and wage brutal war to gain their own ends.

The debate grew heated as Ben Gregory attempted to get some consensus for action.

'We gotta form our own vigilante group. You know the old saw, 'united we stand — divided we fall'.'

'How can we stand together, Ben Gregory? We're small farmers scattered around the county. We got stock to attend, an' fields to plough an' harvests to bring in. We got no time for vigilante duty.'

Ben Gregory rubbed his big hand across his face as he thought about these issues. It was not an easy role he had taken on himself as the organizer of resistance against the ruthless men who would be riding against them.

28

The wagons rolled along accompanied by the cheerful chatter of female voices and the occasional burst of laughter. Behind the wagon carrying Jennie Fletcher and her girls Kate Prentice held the reins of her buggy loosely and wondered if she would ever again see the young rancher from the Big G. It had come as a shock to realize that the ordinary cowboy she had met at the roadhouse was in reality the owner of the biggest and richest ranch in Lundon County. She thought of her own humble background and smiled wryly.

'I'm a cook in a whorehouse,' she muttered, her words covered up by the rumble of wheels, 'and for all he knows, when I need the money I take turns upstairs.' Wistfully she gazed off into the distance regretting what she knew could never be.

'Kate, pull over,' her Aunt Gertie called. She had been in the buggy with Mrs Hendron and her one remaining son.

Dragged back from her day-dreaming Kate obediently pulled the team to the side of the trail and twisted in the seat to see what was going on behind her.

'It's Mathew, Kate, he's took ill. I thought if we stop and give him a sip of water it might revive him.'

Kate glanced at the boy. He was slumped in his seat looking very pale. She watched as the two women jumped down on to the side of the trail and helped the boy to the ground. Aunt Gertie put a reassuring arm around the boy while Kate handed a canteen to Mrs Hendron. Urged on by Kate's aunt the boy took a few sips.

'Let's go for a little walk.' Gertie said and, with her arm still around the boy, they walked into the trees. Kate heard the sound of someone vomiting. She climbed down beside Mrs Hendron.

'Poor Mathew, I hope it's not serious.'

Mathew's mother smiled back at Kate. 'I'm blaming you, Kate Prentice.'

Kate looked aghast at her neighbour, but Mrs Hendron chuckled.

'It was all those tasty cakes and cookies you baked for the funeral meal. I'm afraid Mathew made a pig of himself. He's fourteen, but he's still only a boy. Every time I looked at him he was scoffing away. Thank you, Kate, for all your efforts to make this a special day for Mathew and myself. Jennie Fletcher told me it was your idea to fetch everyone along. I felt we gave James a lovely send-off.' The older woman reached out and took Kate's hands in hers. 'You know James was especially keen on you?'

'Me, I . . . I don't understand.'

'He often spoke of you. He had plans to get a few head of cattle together and find a little spread. Once he was established he was going to call on you.'

'Mrs Hendron, I never knew. James

never said anything to me.'

'He wouldn't, for he felt he wasn't in a position to offer you anything. That's why he was keen to start up on his own. But until that became a reality he respected you enough to keep his distance.'

'Mrs Hendron, I . . . I don't know what to say. I feel honoured that James felt that way about me. He deserved better.'

'Yes.' Mrs Hendron wiped away a tear. 'I had to tell you all this for James's sake. That's why today your efforts were so precious to me and Mathew and James.'

Kate looked away, too embarrassed to make any reply. She was saved any further conversation by the return of the old woman and her young charge. She could see straight away that Mathew looked much better after his purging session in the bushes.

When they were all aboard again Kate took up the reins, her mind in a turmoil as she mulled over Mrs

Hendron's remarks.

'Looks like we lost our travelling companions,' Gertie observed.

Kate looked up the empty trail and noticed the diminishing of the daylight. 'I guess you're right, Aunt Gertie. Still, it doesn't matter. It's getting late so I can cut across to our place and I'll drop you off and then take Mrs Hendron and Mathew home.'

'Kate.' Mrs Hendron spoke up, 'I would like to thank Jennie and her girls for the effort they made today for James. It was a nice gesture on their part to give up their time.'

'No trouble, Mrs Hendron, we'll still have time for that.' She flicked the reins and the buggy started forward again.

As she drove Kate mulled over what Mrs Hendron had told her about her son, James, and his ambition to start up his own ranch and then come courting her. She had known James Hendron for a goodly part of her life. They had gone to school together. In all that time she had never thought of him as a potential husband. Invariably her thoughts turned again to another young man and her pulse quickened. She knew it was highly improbable that he would ever come courting but nevertheless she could not help indulging in a little day-dreaming.

Behind her she could hear Aunt Gertie talking to Mathew and she smiled. Her aunt would chatter away to the youngster to distract him from his queasiness. The pony trotted on into the gathering dusk. Kate began to recognize familiar landmarks.

'Not far now to the roadhouse,' she called back to her passengers.

At first she was puzzled by the popping sounds that came from some distance away. She cocked her ear.

'Gunshots,' called out Mathew. 'There's some shootin' up ahead.'

Kate hauled on the reins and the buggy slowed to a halt. The little group strained eyes and ears into the gathering darkness. Now that the buggy had halted they could hear better the distant sounds of gunfire. Kate turned and stared back at her passengers.

'Oh no! You don't think they're attacking the roadhouse again?'

Aunt Gertie was standing upright now, gripping the back of the driver's seat. 'Girl, I think you're right. That's where the shooting's coming from.'

Kate raised the reins to start up the pony again when she felt her aunt's hand on her arm.

'Wait, we don't know what we're riding into. It won't do no good if we run into them vigilantes ourselves. What use will a bunch of women be if them gunmen have returned?'

'What about me?'

Kate and her aunt turned to look at Mathew.

'Sorry, Mathew. We got us a good man here to look after us, Kate, but go easy all the same. Come on, young man, you get up here beside Kate. We need your young eyes and ears to warn us of any danger ahead.'

They started out again with Mathew, his illness forgotten in his eagerness to impress the womenfolk, sitting full of importance up beside Kate as she drove cautiously towards the roadhouse.

29

The shooting had stopped. Kate pulled the buggy off the road when she knew they were very close to the roadhouse.

'I'm going ahead on foot,' she said. 'You lot stay here. I know the layout of the buildings. I'm going to sneak up as close as I can and find out what's going on.'

'For God's sake be careful. Remember what happened the last time,' Aunt Gertie admonished her.

Mathew climbed down from the buggy.

'Where are you going?' his mother hissed.

'I'm goin' with Kate.'

'No you are not! I've buried one son today. You stay here with Gertie and me.'

'Aw, Ma!'

Kate put her hand on the boy's

shoulder. 'Mathew, can you drive a buggy?'

'Sure.'

'If anything happens to me you get on that gig, drive hell for leather over to Ben Gregory's place and tell him what's happened.' She could almost see the boy swell with importance.

'Sure thing, Miss Kate. You take care now.'

Leaving her companions Kate walked forward cautiously. She cut through the fields behind the roadhouse. The place was ablaze with lights. Alert for anyone lurking about, she crept forward.

The evening was well advanced by now and the darkness shielded her progress. The smell of tobacco warned her in time. She dropped to a crouch and spotted the cigarette glow as the smoker drew hard on his smoke. This forced her to make a detour but she knew the terrain and gradually was able to come up beside the house. She crouched low and could see into the front yard. As she watched she could hear voices raised in anger. There came the sound of a slap and a man's irritated voice yelled out. A cold fear seized her as she listened. It seemed a repeat of the raid of a few nights ago.

There came the noise of a vehicle approaching. She watched as a gig rolled into the yard. Men spilled out of the front of the house.

'Howdy, Mr Murphy, we got everythin' under control here.'

'Good. Take this rig round the back out of sight an' put all the horses up in the top paddocks. The place has to look as if it's business as usual if the trap is to be sprung.'

Kate saw the big man swing down and with the help of a walking stick limp up the steps and enter the house. He was still giving orders as he went inside and Kate could hear no more but she thought she had heard enough. She did not know whom the raiders were waiting for. The only assumption she could make was that they hoped to catch someone paying Jennie with stolen beeves. If they caught the roadhouse owner in the act of receiving stolen cattle then Murphy would consider himself justified in hanging the brothel keeper.

Slowly she backed away and quickly returned to her anxious companions. In terse sentences she told them what she had heard and seen.

'If you lot agree I'll drop you all off at our place and then drive on over to Ben's and tell him what's going on. He'll know what to do.'

★　★　★

''Damn it, Hal, I don't like it one little bit. You can't go over there all by your lonesome. Every time you get anywhere near Peterstown you get shot at.'

'John, what the hell else is there to do! We can't let those people be slaughtered. I'd never live with myself if I did nothin'. Now you get saddled up an' ride hell for leather to the governor an' tell him what's goin' on down here.

Tell him law an' order has broken down an' the ranchers are takin' the law into their own hands and killin' settlers. Take Francisco with you. In the meantime I'll get over to the roadhouse and warn Jennie. In fact, if she's willin' I'm gonna tell her to come back here. She and her girls can take refuge here till this mess is over.' Hal swung into the saddle. 'Don't let me down, John.'

John Grant watched his brother ride out with deep misgivings. He turned round to find the Mexican, Francisco Gonzales, standing near.

'What is it, Francisco?'

'Boss John, I no like this much.'

'Well that's two of us.'

'I know Ronald Preston. I worked the Lazy M a few seasons. He sure one mean coyotero. Somethin' smells in the hay-barn, Señor John.'

'What you sayin', Francisco?'

'Señor Preston a Murphy man through and through. He not come here to do Boss Hal no favour. He got a bone to fry.'

John turned to stare after his brother. Hal had vanished into the gathering gloom. Somewhere in the murky evening another horse started up and John stared towards the sound. 'Someone goin' out late tonight? I thought the nightriders were already out there.'

'My guess is Harvey Baker. He always comin' and goin' at all odd hours.'

'Baker!' John frowned. He had never liked the surly cowhand but the man did his work efficiently enough.

'Somethin' fishy about that man. Charlie Morton says he see him comin' outta Murphy's once or twice.'

'The hell you say!' John remembered speculating on someone watching the ranch and spying on them. 'Francisco, how you fancy a visit to a cathouse tonight?'

John saw a flash of white teeth in the gloom as the Mexican grinned at him. 'Me, I never pay for my pleasures. I have *señoritas* and *señoras* as be in love with me. But I will go with you and hold your hand for you or your britches.'

'Damn your insolent hide, Francisco. How many men we got that'll ride into Peterstown after Hal? Fellas that ain't afraid of a mite of trouble.'

'Hell, Boss John, they all follow you an' Boss Hal. There's half a dozen that can fire a gun an' not run.'

'Right, Francisco, rout them out. Tell them what's happenin'. We goin' to ride to Jennie Fletcher's.'

'But what about the governor?'

'The hell with the governor, he ain't my type.'

★ ★ ★

Hal let the mare set its own pace as he rode into the deepening gloom of nightfall. There was no hurry for his rescue mission. Ronald Preston had said the vigilantes were to set out in the morning, by which time Hal would have escorted the women away from the roadhouse. After all that had happened he did not expect any difficulty in persuading Jennie and her girls to flee from the impending danger.

30

'Law's-a-mercy, child, what is the matter?' Alice Gregory stared at the distraught face of the young girl who had been hammering on her door.

'I'm sorry to disturb you, Mrs Gregory, but I must speak with Ben. It's very urgent.'

'Ben's not here, child, but do come in. You *are* in a state.'

Kate stared aghast at the older woman. Mrs Gregory was a tall, handsome woman with a full figure and a head of long, dark hair.

'But I must find Ben. Were is he?'

'What's going on, child? You'd better tell me and then I'll see what I can do.'

'The vigilantes have returned. They've taken over Jennie Fletcher's place and are waiting for any as comes along. My guess is they want to catch someone drive up with stolen cattle. Some of the customers pay in livestock. Then they'll more 'n likely hang everyone.'

Mrs Gregory put her hand to her mouth. 'Oh God save us, them poor women! Ben told me all that went on the other night. I can't help you, Kate, Ben's in Peterstown. He called a meeting of the settlers. That's where he is now.'

But Mrs Gregory was talking to an empty doorway. Kate had whirled and climbed back on board her buggy.

'Hey up there,' she yelled and the rig rolled out of the Gregorys' yard with Kate urging the tired pony to make more speed.

Night had properly fallen by the time she saw the lights of Peterstown. The pony's pace had slowed considerably. It had made the long trek across to the Big G in the morning for the funeral of James Hendron, then the same journey back again and then Kate had pushed it hard to get to the Gregorys' place. Now it was valiantly struggling on the last leg of the marathon to make it to Peterstown.

Kate could see the lights blazing from the front of the Sheep Dip. The hitching-rail was crowded with tethered horses. The parking-lot by the side of the saloon was packed with buggies and wagons and farm vehicles. Instinctively she guessed that was where Ben Gregory was to be found. Quickly she leapt down from her own transport and without waiting to tie up the worn-out pony she ran up the steps and pressed into the fetid atmosphere of the Sheep Dip.

Slightly bewildered by the racket coming out of the crowded room Kate hesitated by the door. The air of the saloon was foggy with tobacco smoke that mingled with the high odour of unwashed bodies. Anxiously Kate scanned the room for any sign of Ben Gregory. Almost immediately she spotted him, for he was standing on a chair at the back of the saloon.

'Ben,' she yelled, and began to wave

her arm high in the air while at the same time pushing into the crowd.

Once men realized a young girl was trying to elbow her way forward they gave way but not without some banter.

'Buy you a drink, missy?'

'Does you pa know you're out tonight?'

'Over here, miss, I'm the best kisser in the county.'

One or two already knew the girl and called to her by name but Kate pushed on.

'I must speak to Ben.'

'Ben, your daughter's here. She's come to take you home.'

Fortunately for Kate, Ben recognized her. Realizing that something was amiss he jumped down and met the girl inside a circle of onlookers.

'Oh, Ben, they've come back. You must do something. They're going to hang everybody. Please come quickly.'

'You mean the vigilantes?'

Breathlessly Kate poured out her story to the big man. When she finished he put his arm round her shoulder and guided her back to the place where he had addressed the crowd.

'Stay close to me,' he instructed Kate. Then stepped up on to the chair and raised his hands for silence. 'Friends, it has started. Kate has just told me the vigilantes have taken over Jennie Fletcher's roadhouse an' are even now out there lyin' in wait for patrons so they can hang them along with Jennie and her girls.'

Before he could continue there was a mighty roar from the crowded bar. Men were shaking their fists in the air and calling for vengeance. Many had been drinking the Sheep Dip's potent liquor and were fired up with Dutch courage. In vain Ben held up his arms and tried to calm the crowd.

'We gotta do this right,' he yelled. We can't go out there like a mob. Let's organize ourselves.'

It was a vain plea. Men were already pouring out through the door and racing for wagons and buggies and saddle-horses.

'Wait,' Ben Gregory called again, but his words were lost as the patrons of the Sheep Dip fought each other to vacate the saloon and ride to wreak vengeance on the vigilantes hired by the Institute of Wyoming Ranchers.

There was no stopping them now. Their blood was fired up with alcohol and the thought of meting out retribution for the years of repression and harassment they had suffered at the hands of their rich and prosperous rancher neighbours. They flung themselves on to horse and vehicle and the vengeful flood of excited men began the exodus from the town.

★   ★   ★

The roadhouse looked unusually quiet as Hal rode up the approach road. He counted three horses tied up front that indicated at least three customers inside. Hal wondered how they would react when he rode up and told Jennie to load all her girls back into the wagon with his invitation for them to take refuge at the Big G. He smiled wryly to himself as he recalled how his cowpunchers had hung around the girls after the funeral.

'There's one bunch of fellas as will be pleased to welcome our guests,' he mused. Then wondered how the work at the Big G would fare with so many females around, distracting his cowpunchers.

He dismounted and tied up his mare beside the other mounts.

'Goddamn it, I sure hope Jennie don't put up too many objections to my plan,' he muttered. Then he pushed open the sagging door and grimaced as the bottom grated across the floorboards.

31

Hal looked around in some surprise. Contrary to his expectations of the roadhouse being empty the bar was crowded. Men were sitting at the tables with drinks and smokes. A few card-games were in progress. Other men hung around the bar and some were on the stairs that led up to the chambers of delights. All the eyes in the room swivelled towards the newcomer.

Hal nodded a greeting, which was not returned. After surveying the room he walked to the bar and got his second shock. He was expecting to see Jennie serving. Instead, a heavy-built man with partly healed cuts on his face was watching Hal approach. Hal halted, his hand going instinctively to his holster.

'I wouldn't, cowboy.' Stump Murphy's hand was curled around a

Greener lying on the bar top, aimed at Hal's midriff.

There was sudden movement all around and a forest of guns appeared as the men in the room brought out weapons that had been concealed when Hal had walked into the roadhouse.

'If he as much as twitches a finger towards those guns of his, every man in the room has my permission to fire.'

Murphy tried to smile but his broken teeth and partly healed lips spoiled the effect. In spite of the danger he was in Hal felt a small glimmer of satisfaction as he saw the damage he had wrought on the big Irishman.

'Just dropped by for a drink,' he said conversationally. 'Wasn't plannin' on hijackin' the joint. You expandin' your business interests into this neck of the woods?'

'Get his weapons,' Murphy growled.

Someone moved up behind Hal and removed his side-arm and the pistol concealed in his back holster. When he was sure Hal was disarmed the big man limped from behind the bar. Hal noted the man's bandaged foot and hand as he picked up a walking-stick and shuffled into the room.

'Looks like you had a wrestle with a trestle,' Hal jibed.

The Irishman did not answer but Hal saw a flicker of anger stir behind those cruel eyes. He planted himself before Hal and stared hard at the cowboy.

'You have caused me a mite of trouble, fella. In the past the men who stood against me ended up dead.' Again Murphy tried that distorted sneer with his damaged mouth. 'Fella name of Harry Grant tried to derail my scheme to put paid to the rustlin' in this county. I sorta recall readin' about the funeral in the local paper.' His eyebrows rose as he stared at Hal. 'Any relation to you?'

Hal's anger surged. 'You son of a bitch, you're a coward and murderer.' He wanted to punch that sneering face but bided his time. With a dozen or so guns trained on him he would be blasted to ribbons before he could get near enough to do any damage. 'What have you done with Jennie an' her girls?' he asked instead.

'Oh, don't worry, they're safe and sound. We got them stashed outside in the barn. I was waitin' for you to come along an' join the party. When I finish with you, Jennie Fletcher and her girls are goin' to another sorta party. We're organizin' a necktie party for them. So the sooner I deal with you the more time they'll have to hang around.'

This brought titters from the hard-cases in the room. Hal quickly scanned the faces and was not surprised to see Ronald Preston among them.

'Howdy, Preston, you sure suckered me in. I always figured you for a connivin' coyote. Murderin' from hidin' and hangin' women tells me how brave you all are. This place is crawlin' with every sort of low-life as snuck out from under a rock.'

With surprising speed Murphy's cane whipped up and struck Hal a stinging blow across the cheek. Instinctively Hal lunged forward but something hit him in the back of the head and he stumbled to the floor. He glared balefully up at the saloon owner.

'I said once you were a coward, Murphy. An' this is the second time I make the claim. You're a coward and a murderer.'

'Coward, eh?' Murphy's eyes were glittering with rage. 'No one ever called me that before an' lived.'

'You're a coward, Murphy, an' all these men know it.' Hal's voice dripped with contempt. 'They're only here because you pay them. Without the money these men wouldn't spit on you if you were on fire. You'll always be remembered as Murphy the Gutless. You couldn't face me man to man. You're a no-good back-shooter and even now you need a score of gunmen to handle one little old cowpoke.'

Hal could see his taunts were having their effect. Murphy's face contorted as the man made a great effort to control his anger.

'You think I'm afraid of a young upstart like you,' Murphy ground out. 'We'll see.' He nodded to the men nearest. 'Get him on his feet.'

Hal was hauled upright.

'Give me his gun.'

Hal did not know what to expect as the man holding his weapons handed the Colt over. Murphy hefted the weapon.

'Man to man,' he said, 'in an even fight.'

Then he pointed the gun and suddenly fired. The shot was deafening in the confined space. The bullet entered the top of Hal's boot and exited into the wooden floor. Hal yelped and snatched his foot off the floor. But for the men holding him he would have fallen.

'Goddamn!' he swore as he felt the crushing pain in his wounded foot.

'Has to be an even fight, you said. I got a bum foot, now you got a bum foot. Makes it more even, don't it? Bring him over here.'

Hal was dragged to one of the tables, unable to put his injured foot on the ground.

'Hold his hand down on the top,' Murphy instructed.

They spread Hal's hand on the tabletop. Hal guessed there would be another shooting and braced himself to withstand the additional pain. Instead Murphy reversed the Colt, raised it up, then brought the butt down with all his force on the knuckles of the out-stretched hand. In spite of his resolve Hal could not suppress a groan as he felt the bones in his hand break under the blow. Murphy stepped back and tossed the gun to the floor.

'Now, we're even, cowboy. You got a busted mitt an' I got a busted mitt. How does it feel?' As he spoke Murphy's big fist came round in a sudden swing and hit Hal in the face. Hal's head was jolted on his neck and he felt as if he had been hit with a hand sledge. He tried to back away but he put his weight on his injured foot and with a gasp of pain stumbled to the floor. There was an excited yell from the men.

'That's it, boss, beat the daylights outta the sonabitch!'

The big man stood glaring down at his victim. 'Just thought you might as well know. If, as is unlikely, you look like gettin' the upper hand, my foreman, Ronald Preston, has orders to shoot you. He won't kill you. Just disable you so's you can hang alongside those whores you seem so fond of.'

Hal saw the man's feet shuffle closer and guessed he would be stomped if he stayed where he was. Hal wasn't even sure he could stand. Pain lanced through his body from his broken hand and wounded foot. On top of that the unexpected punch from Murphy had dazed him. He tried to roll away but wasn't quick enough and a boot hit him in the temple.

This time lights went off in his head. He knew he had to regain his feet if he were to stand any chance of surviving.

In desperation he put his injured hand on the floor and tried to lever himself to his feet. He almost cried out as the broken bones grated together. Then Murphy's boot caught him in the ear and he fell on to his back with a jolt that almost shook loose his hold on consciousness.

The violent movement drove excruciating pain through every part of his body. Waves of dizziness washed over him. In desperation he lashed out with his good foot and managed to hook Murphy behind the calf as the big man moved in on him again. It was a lucky move and the big man, off balance on his injured foot, fell with a resounding thud to the floor.

The crowd in the barroom were screaming for the fighters to continue. They were savage men and witnessing a fight roused the beast in them.

Hal groaned and painfully scrabbled to his feet. He could put no pressure on his injured foot and was trying to balance on the other as he stood. Then he saw the brutal face of his attacker before him. He drove his fist into the man's jaw.

The blow hurt his hand as his knuckles ground into teeth. Murphy screamed and flung himself at Hal. Powerful arms closed around Hal and the big man began to squeeze. His face was inches from Hal. The teeth and lips were a bloody mess where Hal's fist had reopened the original wounds inflicted during the fight in the funeral parlour.

'This is the end, cowboy,' the big man gritted out, and blood and spit sprayed on to Hal's face.

The youngster felt the pressure building in his ribs as his opponent tightened his grip. There was a red glaze forming before his eyes as his breathing was constricted. His wounds throbbed and he felt the beginnings of despair sapping at his will to fight on.

He hardly registered the shots from outside the building. The gunmen in the room scrambled to the windows, guns at the ready. He could hear shouting from outside and then the room exploded with gunfire as the men inside answered the shots coming from outside.

32

'Kill the sons of bitches!' someone yelled.

The noise from exploding guns was deafening inside the barroom as men smashed at windows to clear the glass and began to return fire.

A bemused Hal was poised in his own little world of pain and constriction as Murphy retained his crushing grip and shouted out to his men to kill everything that moved outside.

'Die, you bastard,' he yelled into Hal's face.

Hal imagined he was dead already and this was hell. It was, he imagined, a punishment for killing James Hendron.

Guns fired continuously and bullets splintered window frames and ricocheted inside the room. Already one or two men were lying on the floor cursing as they nursed bullet wounds. Still the noise and fumes built up and Hal wanted nothing more than to curl up somewhere and bring ease to his pain-racked body. Instead he drove his knee up into his tormentor's groin. The man grunted but the crushing pressure on Hal's chest was unrelenting. An iron band was slowly crushing his chest and lungs. Any minute he expected his ribs to cave in. The pressure was becoming unbearable. Then he began hallucinating.

He was remembering the first time he had come to this roadhouse. He had killed the men responsible for his father's murder. Then Scoote had fired in through the window at him and hit him in the arm. Hal had fired at the window and the killer had fled. Now Hal sought out the window and twisted his body towards the place. The movement panicked Murphy, who was thinking there was no more fight left in Hal. He had killed men like this before by using his brute strength to crush the life from them.

'Someone kill this sonabitch!' he yelled. But his words were lost in the storm of gunfire raking the building.

Hal drove his wounded foot into the floor and pressed forward. The agony he precipitated by his action cleared his mind for a moment. Again he pressed forward, unaware that with each slight movement he left a bloody print on the floor.

He saw the window then. A man was crouching to one side of it, reaching out with his Colt without exposing himself and firing blindly into the yard. Bullets shattered chips of wood from the frame. The man withdrew his hand and reloaded. Hal pushed again — his injured foot a white-hot ball of agony. Slowly, ever so slowly, the big man holding him in the rib-crushing grip gave ground. The man's face was red with his exertions and sweat dripped down his face and mingled with the blood. Something had to give and it was Murphy.

He tried to stop Hal pushing against

him but Hal was gripped by one single-minded idea. He was heading for that window and while his head swam in dizzy waves and excruciating pain drove up into his leg every time he put his wounded foot to the ground and his lungs were a fire of white-hot agony he pressed steadily forward.

Inch by painful inch he moved and each bloody footprint was won at a terrible price in pain and exertion. He was determined he would not give up now. With one last heroic heave they crashed against the broken window.

Hal felt the man holding him stiffen and his body jerked convulsively as bullets from outside found a target. The big man opened his mouth and a glob of blood gushed on to Hal's face. Murphy's eyes were wide and staring. His mouth was working but no words were forming. The terrible grip slackened and then both men fell to the floor.

Hal lay where he was. The firing had not slackened. Men were yelling out and firing into the yard. Hal did not want to move. Then he imagined Kate held prisoner with the women, awaiting execution by Murphy's vigilantes. With one huge effort he heaved and Murphy's dead weight rolled from him.

The man who had been firing through that fateful window was busy reloading. Hal moved forward and gripped the weapon with his good hand. The man looked up in surprise. Unable to use his wounded hand Hal did the only thing possible. He drove his head into the face of the startled man in front of him. He threw every last shed of desperate effort into that forward thrust. The man's head banged against the wall. Unseen by either of them a protruding splinter drove up into the back of the man's neck. He died instantly.

Hal fell on top of the dead man who was still holding on to the gun, and began hitting him with his injured hand. Only after several agonizing blows did he realize the man was not fighting back. Hal found himself lying on the floor beside two dead men and in possession of a loaded revolver.

Slowly he twisted round to face into the room. The massive bulk of the dead Murphy shielded him from the men defending the roadhouse. Hal looked for and spotted Ronald Preston. His hand was shaking so badly he had to rest the butt of the gun on top of his dead opponent. Preston was standing by the doorway. He had kicked the door open and two men were lying on the floor, firing out into the yard. Preston was yelling instructions and encouragement to the gunmen.

Hal sighted on the foreman and squeezed the trigger. At that range he couldn't miss. The bullet took Preston high in the chest and punched him into the open doorway. Like his master he was instantly hit by incoming fire. He staggered back into the room and fell across the marksmen lying on the floor. With all the noise and confusion no one guessed but that the foreman had been slain by the attackers.

Hal looked around the room, sighted on his next target and began to kill the gunmen. They died one by one, mostly unaware their assailant was in the room with them.

33

'Damn you, Hal, I just wish you'd listen to me for once. I may be the younger brother but I got a damn sight more sense than you.'

Hal grinned down as his brother's distraught face. He was sitting on a two-seater buggy with his foot swathed in bandages and propped up on the footboard. His arm was in a sling and he was inexpertly handling the reins one-handed.

'Little brother, this is somethin' I have to do. It can't wait another day.'

'When Doc patched you up he said you had to rest for at least a week before usin' that foot.'

'I ain't got a week, John, and anyway I'm not usin' my foot. It's restin' on the board.'

'Hal, it's been two days since we carted you back from Jennie Fletcher's.

When I saw you lyin' there with all that blood I sure as hell thought you were dead.'

'You know, John, I think you put a hex on me. You told me every time I went over Peterstown I got a bullet in me.'

'An' I'm tellin' you the same thing now.'

'Tell Ma I'll try an' be back for supper.' Hal flicked the reins and the well-schooled horse trotted forward, leaving Hal's worried brother glaring after him.

Hal had lain on his back for one day only after he was brought back from the gory arena of Jennie Fletcher's road-house. John had brought him up to date on the happenings of that dreadful night of slaughter.

As far as he was concerned Kate Prentice was the hero. She had ridden through the night and warned Ben Gregory about the raiders. The homesteaders had surrounded the building after releasing Jennie and her girls held prisoner out in the barn. Believing that only Murphy's vigilantes remained in the roadhouse they had poured fire into the building to dislodge the gunmen. With Murphy and his foreman dead and several of the raiders killed by Hal they had quickly surrendered.

The angry homesteaders were for hanging the remnants of the raiders but by that time John Grant had arrived and added his voice to that of Ben Gregory to prevent any more killing. Instead the dispirited raiders were loaded on to a wagon and driven to Toska for the marshal there to deal with. Now Hal had one last errand and refused to postpone it, in spite of his brother's protestations.

As the light rig bounced along the bumpy road Hal tried to ignore the jolting his foot was taking. He pursed his lips against the discomfort and even urged the pony to go faster.

The drive seemed to take days and he was mightily relieved when he neared his destination. Only when he was guiding the buggy down the rutted path to the homestead did he begin to have doubts about the wisdom of his mission. But he had come this far and he felt he had to go through with it. He pulled up in the yard and contemplated the effort of alighting with his throbbing foot. As he struggled to the side of the buggy an elderly woman came round the side of the house. She was carrying a hoe and her face lit up when she saw who her visitor was.

'Hal Grant, by all that's holy, I would have thought you'd had enough of this neck of the woods.'

'Aunt Gertie, maybe you'd excuse me gettin' down. It's a mite tricky for the moment.'

'Kate, we got ourselves a visitor,' the old woman yelled in a startlingly strident voice.

'I'll be there in moment,' a muffled voice called from inside the cabin.

'How's the gardenin' comin' on?' Hal asked while he waited.

Before he got an answer Kate

appeared at the cabin door. She was trying to straighten her dress. And her golden hair was in a tangle. Her face was flushed and a smudge of flour on her forehead announced what she had been doing when Hal rode up.

Hal stared at the young girl and felt his heart miss a beat. This was why he had driven all the way over from the Big G and now he was here he was speechless as he contemplated the lovely young girl staring back up at him. The temerity of what he had to say to her temporarily overwhelmed him.

'Kate,' he said tentatively and his throat dried up. He did not see Aunt Gertie sidle indoors with a knowing grin on her wrinkled old face

'Hal, how is your foot? I was so worried about you.'

'I . . . came to thank you, Kate for what you did. If you hadn't gone for Ben I don't think I would have survived.'

She smiled up at him and his aches

and pains and worries seemed to lessen under the radiance of that smile. He made an awkward attempt to get down and winced as he jarred his foot.

'Oh, Hal you're still in pain. Let me help.'

She reached for his hand and he felt the soft warmth of her touch.

'I came to ask if you would come for a drive with me,' he said diffidently. 'There's something I want to ask you.'

Again she gave him that radiant smile. 'Of course, Hal. I'll just get my shawl.' She turned and walked back to the cabin.

Hal eased himself into the seat of the buggy. He heard the horse coming down the path and turned to watch the rider approach. The man rode slouched in the saddle with his hat pulled low, obscuring his face. Hal assumed it was a neighbour coming to visit. Then the man looked up, raised his Winchester and pointed it at Hal.

'Mr high an' mighty Hal Grant, I been waitin' for you to show up.'

'Harvey Baker,' Hal said puzzled. 'What the hell you doin' here?'

'Come to settle up some old debts. You killed Murphy and Preston. You see, I was workin' for them. Murphy promised me a job with the Lazy M. I was bein' paid good money to keep him informed of your comin's and goin's. Somehow your brother found out an' sacked me. Wouldn't even pay me the wages he owed me. I knew you was sweet on the whorehouse girl so I sat about waitin' for you. I was sure you would turn up eventually.'

'What you want, Harvey? I can pay you now.'

Hal made a movement as if to reach into his pocket. The shot from the rifle took splinters from the headboard of the buggy.

'Just throw down that pistol nice an' easy. I don't want to kill you in front of the females but I will if you give me any bother.'

Hal carefully extracted his Colt and dropped it into the dust of the yard.

'Now that hide-out gun I know you wear.'

Hal swore silently and did as he was told. The second weapon joined the first one in the dust. He heard the door of the cabin open and saw Harvey's eyes shift to a place behind him.

'Howdy, miss, I'm takin' your boyfriend for a little ride. Don't make a fuss or I'll put a slug in him.'

Hal looked over his shoulder. Kate was standing beside the rig, her face pale with her shawl in her hand.

'Go back in the house, Kate,' he said. 'I'm sorry about this.'

'So am I, Hal. I was looking forward to our little ride.' She looked beyond Hal to the rider on the horse. 'I just want to say goodbye,' she pleaded.

'Yeah, but hurry up. I wanna be on my way.'

Kate reached her hands up towards Hal. Her eyes were tearful. With her pale face Hal thought she was the very image of an alabaster saint he had once seen in a church. The saint was proffering a posy of flowers towards the divine presence and had a look of tearful supplication in the beautiful carved face. Now Kate reached up — the shawl she had brought out to wear dangling from her hands.

'I love you,' Hal could say the words he found so difficult before he felt the presence of death in the shape of Harvey Baker approach. Through her tears she smiled and he took her hands in his and felt the hard shape of a gun butt concealed in the shawl.

'I love you, Hal Grant. You come back soon and take me for that drive.'

He turned with the ancient pistol in his hand — the one Kate had used in the roadhouse several days ago. His first shot nicked the horse's ear and ricocheted from the pommel. The horse jerked and jumped to one side, throwing Baker's answering shot wide. This damn thing fires low, thought Hal as he triggered another shot. He over-compensated and hit Baker high in the shoulder.

The man was fighting his bucking mount as he tried to bring the Winchester to bear. He grunted as Hal's bullet hit him but stayed upright. A rifle boomed from the house as Kate's aunt stood in the doorway and fired at the mounted man. Hal fired again and the bullet smashed into Harvey's hand as he tried to work the mechanism of the rifle. Then Aunt Gertie got her range and her next shot hit Baker in the chest. Hal fired again but Baker was tumbling from his horse. He was dead before he hit the ground from the terrible wound the old woman's bullet had inflicted in his chest. The horse, freed of its rider, wheeled and fled back up the path. Hal turned back to the girl staring wide-eyed up at him.

'Kate, will you marry me?' he blurted out.

Then he could say no more for she had clambered up beside him and, with her arms wrapped round him, pressed her lips hard against his.

We do hope that you have enjoyed reading this large print book.

Did you know that all of our titles are available for purchase?

We publish a wide range of high quality large print books including:
Romances, Mysteries, Classics
General Fiction
Non Fiction and Westerns

Special interest titles available in large print are:
The Little Oxford Dictionary
Music Book, Song Book
Hymn Book, Service Book

Also available from us courtesy of Oxford University Press:
Young Readers' Dictionary
(large print edition)
Young Readers' Thesaurus
(large print edition)

For further information or a free brochure, please contact us at:
Ulverscroft Large Print Books Ltd.,
The Green, Bradgate Road, Anstey,
Leicester, LE7 7FU, England.
Tel: (00 44) **0116 236 4325**
Fax: (00 44) **0116 234 0205**

Other titles in the
Linford Western Library:

FIND MADIGAN!

Hank J. Kirby

Bronco Madigan was the top man in the US Marshals' Service — and now he was missing. Working on the most important and most dangerous mission he'd ever been assigned, he'd disappeared into the gunsmoke. Everything pointed to him being one of the many dead bodies left along the bloody trail. Even his sidekick, Kimble, was almost ready to give up the search, but the Chief's orders were very clear: 'Find Madigan . . . at all costs!'

MISFIT LIL GETS EVEN

Chap O'Keefe

While Silver Vein's citizens watch 'Misfit Lil' shine in a gala shooting match, Yuma Nat Hawkins and his gang rob the bank and gun down the depleted opposition in cold blood. Patrick 'Preacher' Kilkieran witnesses the robbery, but keeps his distance — and is soon striking a mysterious deal with a renegade Indian before fleeing town. But it's Kilkieran's brutal assault on Lil's friend Estelle that compels her to vow retribution and track him down . . .

ON THE WAPITI RANGE

Owen G. Irons

When wapiti hunters arrive on Lee Trent's Green River preserve, they bring trouble by carrying too many guns into his peaceful realm. If that weren't enough, they are also holding prisoner a beautiful madwoman in a windowless wagon. The elk hunters' presence threatens to bring Lee into conflict with the Cheyenne Indians, and his neighbours. Then disaster follows when the hunt becomes a slaughter. And Lee must handle the invaders by himself if he is to recover his mountain domain.

ARIZONA SHOWDOWN

Corba Sunman

Travis Jordan was a bounty hunter with his own reasons for turning his back on normal life. Then someone appeared from his past with a plea for help. Family duty reached for him, which he could not ignore, and he returned to his home range. But once he drew his pistol, he would be unable to holster it until the last shot in a bitter clean-up had been fired. It was kill-or-be-killed — and he was resolute that he would win . . .